AN UNEXPECTED ENCOUNTER

Miss Victoria Marsh has an unexpected encounter in the church with a handsome, but disagreeable, soldier who is recuperating from a grievous leg injury. Major Toby Highcliff believes himself to be a useless cripple, but meeting Victoria changes everything. Will he be able to keep her safe from the evil that stalks the neighbourhood and convince her he is the ideal man for her?

FENELLA MILLER

AN UNEXPECTED ENCOUNTER

Complete and Unabridged

LINFORD
Leicester

First published in Great Britain in 2010

First Linford Edition
published 2013

A catalogue record for this book is available
from the British Library.

ISBN 978–1–4448–1648–8

Published by
F. A. Thorpe (Publishing)
Anstey, Leicestershire

Set by Words & Graphics Ltd.
Anstey, Leicestershire
Printed and bound in Great Britain by
T. J. International Ltd., Padstow, Cornwall

This book is printed on acid-free paper

1

Miss Victoria Marsh was walking briskly down the narrow lane that led from the grounds of Butterfield Hall to the small village of Bentley. It was a perfect summer's day. She paused to listen to the nightingales singing in a nearby coppice and watched the sky-larks high above as the sun warmed her face. It was far too long since she'd had the freedom to enjoy such simple pleasures.

She shuddered as she recalled the past weeks, she'd thought that at any moment her only relative was going to depart this life, leaving her bereft.

She frowned. Was it not a lovely day, had she not the morning to herself for the first time in weeks? She must stop dwelling on the past and enjoy the present. Aunt Martha was almost recovered and she was going to spend an hour with her bosom bow. She couldn't wait to catch up on the local news, Marybeth always had the latest on this, the vicarage was the hub of village.

She'd not been walking more than a mile when something sharp pressed into the sole of her foot. Botheration! How was it possible for a stone to have worked its way in? Spying a convenient log on the side of the lane she hobbled across and sat down in order to remove her half-kid boot.

She emptied the pebble out — what a small thing to cause so much discomfort. Whilst lacing her boot she glanced across the lane at a flurry of sparrows as they flew into the hedge.

Her fingers stilled. Wasn't that something shiny hidden amongst the leaves? Quickly tying the bow she dropped her skirts and hurried across to investigate. Crouching down she rummaged into the foliage until her fingers settled on what she had seen. Good gracious! How did a gold and diamond necklace come to be tossed so casually aside? Victoria held the object up and the stones sparkled in the sunlight. This was no doubt a valuable item, someone must be desperate to have it returned.

She dropped the necklace into her reticule and pulled the drawstring tight. A note must be sent to the local magistrate, Sir John Farnham, she would pen it whilst visiting her friend. Such excitement, perhaps there would be a reward? It was doubtful that the necklace had been lost by its owner, it was far more likely it had been stolen in another of the burglaries that were rife in the neighbourhood. The thieves must have carelessly dropped the item in their hurry to escape.

She continued her walk towards the village revelling in the solitude. The sound of horses approaching caused her to step out of the lane; she did not deliberately hide herself, but the trees she was standing under all but obscured her outline. When she saw who was approaching she pressed herself further into the shadows. The ramshackle, unshaven individuals were obviously searching for the missing item. If they discovered her, her life might well be in danger.

These two unsavoury felons were searching the hedgerows for their lost loot. They halted a few yards from her. Her heart thudded painfully. What if they saw her lurking in the undergrowth? Should she run for her life or remain still and hope for the best?

Then they moved off apparently unaware they were being observed. With a sigh of relief she slipped out from behind the trees and almost ran the remaining mile to the village. At no time did she return to the lane, instead she made her way across the meadows and over the stile to arrive in Bentley through the wicket gate that led into the church yard.

She paused amidst the gravestones to adjust her bonnet and shake out the dust and debris from her hem. She wiped her brow with her handkerchief as her breathing returned to normal. It would not do to appear looking dishevelled, the tabbies would take note and it would be all around the village by teatime.

On impulse she decided to go into the church and send up a prayer of thanks to the Almighty for the safe delivery of her beloved aunt. The interior of the old building was cool and quiet, it was, as expected, quite deserted. She walked down the central aisle and dipped her head in reverence. Moving into her usual pew she knelt quietly and clasped her hands.

Five minutes passed before she pushed herself on to the bench satisfied the Lord had heard her prayers. She watched the dust motes floating in the golden glow from the window, it had been far too long since she had been able to spend time in this hallowed building. A slight sound to her left caused her heart to skitter, her head shot sideways to meet the eyes of an equally startled gentleman. He'd been hidden in the shadows at the far side of the building.

He stood up clumsily sending a stack of books tumbling to the flagstones. He was muttering words sounding suspiciously like curses as he attempted to retrieve them. Victoria could see at once that he was lame, his right leg seemed unable to bend. Immediately she hurried over to assist.

'Please, sir, let me pick them up for you. I am so sorry that I shocked you, I had no idea there was anyone else in the church.'

The gentleman seemed annoyed. His fierce expression almost made her regret her offer. Quickly she scooped up the books to replace them on the side table that stood at the end of the pew. By this time he'd managed to prise himself up. He was glaring down at her. In spite of his obvious infirmity it detracted nothing from his physical presence. He must be a veteran recovering from an injury received in one of the ghastly battles that had taken place so recently in Spain.

Keeping her head demurely lowered she curtsied neatly. 'I know it is not proper for me to introduce myself, but as there is no one here to do it for me, I am Miss Victoria Marsh. I am delighted to meet you, I believe you must be a stranger in these parts.'

She glanced nervously through her lashes, waiting for to him to tell her who he was. Something flickered in his eyes, she wasn't certain if it was annoyance or amusement. Then he inclined his head an inch. His voice was deep, authoritative, it fitted his appearance.

'Toby Highcliff, at your service, Miss Marsh.'

He didn't add that he was delighted to make her acquaintance. Without thinking she blurted out her thoughts. 'Are you not an officer? I thought you must have been injured at Badajoz, or somewhere similar.'

His expression became even frostier. 'You are impertinent, miss. Pray excuse me, I have business elsewhere.' He inclined his head a fraction and with surprising speed for a man with his disability, vanished down the aisle. Fortunately she'd left the door ajar and there was nothing there to impede his progress.

She scowled after him. No doubt he was in pain, but there was no excuse for incivility. She stood for a few moments regaining her composure. Her lips twitched, was she not in the house of the Lord? The irascible gentleman, Mr Highcliff, must be forgiven. Her eyes sparkled; but he wouldn't be forgotten, that was for certain.

He was just leaving the churchyard when she reached the door. He was elegantly dressed, his top coat of dark-blue superfine, his inexpressibles beige and his top boots polished to a high shine. His hair was more black than brown and if she remembered rightly, his eyes had been a most unusual shade somewhere between grey and pale blue.

She must not stand dithering and

daydreaming about an unexpected encounter with a curmudgeonly gentleman, she had errands to run and if she intended to visit Marybeth she had better get about her business at once. She was determined to return in time to share a mid-day meal with her great aunt.

★ ★ ★

Toby continued his lopsided march until he was certain the young lady could no longer see him; exhausted by his effort, he leant against a tree to recover his equilibrium. Perspiration trickled down his cheeks, he rummaged in his pocket to remove his handkerchief. Dr Clark had warned him not to overdo things until his leg was fully mended. What had possessed him to stride off in that ridiculous fashion?

His face relaxed, for the first time in many months he felt there was a glimmer of light at the end of a very dark tunnel. The girl's lovely smile had unexpectedly knocked him off balance for a moment and her instantly recognising him as an ex-soldier had added to his discomfiture. His military career was over, his leg would never recover sufficiently for him to be able to resume his command. He had only his half pay and the small amount he'd accumulated in prize money between himself and destitution.

He was staying with his brother-in-law, Sir John Farnham, but could not stay there indefinitely.

They had a nursery full of children to provide for and only a modest income with which to do it. He must come up with a way of earning his own living, it was his intention to remain with his sister only until the following weekend, they must be heartily sick of seeing his long face in their happy home. He must discover who the young lady was when he returned. It was a small community, Celia was bound to know every well bred young lady who lived in the vicinity.

The handsome gelding John had loaned him was waiting patiently outside; as his right leg no longer bent at the knee Toby had some difficulty when remounting his horse but had almost mastered the procedure. Another ten days and he would have it perfected and would be able to leave. As he cantered home he wondered if his fervent prayers had been answered in a way he'd never considered. Was Miss Marsh to be his salvation? He shook his head — miracles were not for the likes of him.

* * *

Victoria had quite forgotten the expensive necklace she carried in her bag as Mr Highcliff dominated her thoughts. He was unknown to her but Marybeth would know all about him. She cut short her shopping expedition in order to hurry to the vicarage. Her friend greeted her at the door.

'Victoria, I cannot tell you how glad I am to see you. It must mean that Mrs

Winterton is sufficiently recovered to allow you to leave her alone.'

'You're quite correct, and I thank God she was spared. She is with her seamstress, determined to renew her wardrobe.' Victoria laughed. 'I cannot imagine why an octogenarian should choose to dress in the first stare of fashion. Indeed, it's only at her behest that my wardrobe is so a la mode. I should be quite happy to continue wearing what I have.'

'But if you did so I should not be nearly so well dressed myself! You're the envy of the village, a veritable fashion plate every time you come to visit us lesser folk.'

Arm in arm the two girls ran inside. Mrs Peters, Marybeth's mother, greeted Victoria with enthusiasm. 'My dear, how lovely to see you and on such a fine day too. Our prayers have been with you these last few weeks, truly it is nothing short of a miracle that your aunt has recovered.'

Victoria curtsied. 'It is, ma'am, I was

reluctant to leave her this morning but she insisted. However I intend to be back by midday, so I do not have more than an hour to spend here, more's the pity.'

'Then I shall not hold you back, my dear, I shall have refreshments sent up to you.'

Once in the privacy of her friend's apartment Victoria turned eagerly to her. 'Marybeth, I encountered the most unpleasant gentleman in church just now. He was abominably rude, I did not like him one bit.'

Marybeth clapped her hands. 'You've met Major Highcliff, he's staying with the squire. He was sorely injured and almost lost his leg. Lady Farnham is his only living relative, he has been recuperating with them these past few weeks, no one has dared to waylay him. You must be the first.'

'How is that? What has he done to frighten away the matrons with eligible daughters?'

'He rides past looking to neither right

nor left, his face so grim, and he does not come into society at all. I should not have had the courage to speak to him.'

Victoria giggled. 'But you must admit Marybeth, for all his ill-humour, he is a prodigiously handsome gentleman. He must be two yards tall at least, and then there's the width of his shoulders — well, all I can say is that he all but blocked out the light from the church door when he eventually exited.'

It wasn't until Victoria was on her way home she recalled the incident with the two unkempt men and the precious property she had secreted in her reticule. How fortuitous that she should come across this particular item today. She almost skipped back down the drive. Now she had the perfect excuse to visit Sir John and discover more about Major Highcliff, there was something about this gentleman that wrung her heartstrings. He had a sadness in his expression that called out for her to offer him her friendship and support. She had once looked like that, then dearest Aunt Martha had come to her rescue. Now she would do the same for him, she was certain he was as lost as she had been three years ago.

2

Toby clattered into the yard and dismounted in his usual awkward fashion. He was aware that both staff and visitors viewed him with pity, a broken man with no future, dependent on the good offices of his relatives for his very existence.

John was leaving as he entered by the front door. 'Toby, just the man I wanted to see. There has been another burglary, this time at the home of Lord Lever. I'm going to visit some of my neighbours and see if they will assist me in trying to capture these villains.'

'Why are you telling me? I can offer you advice, but my active days are over. I am little more than a useless cripple, sometimes I wish I had perished in the accident.' The shock on his brother-in-law's face made him feel ashamed of his sharp words. 'I beg your pardon, John, I am in a fit of the blue devils today. I would be happy to give you my advice when you have assembled your informal militia.'

'Good man, Celia is waiting to speak to you, some domestic detail or other. Are you sure you would not like to accompany me?'

Toby shook his head, he hated to be obliged to reveal his infirmity. Until he had completely mastered the mount and dismount from his horse he would ride alone. 'Not this time, but I will, of course, be part of the group when it is assembled. My rifle might well prove invaluable.'

He limped up to the marble steps and nodded at the waiting footman. He was greeted immediately by his sister's delighted call.

'Toby, I have been waiting this age for you to return. We have been invited to an informal party at Buckfast House on Friday. Lord Lever has included a note addressed to you.' She handed him the parchment square and he broke the blob of sealing wax. He quickly scanned what was written inside with a sinking heart. Celia was waiting expectantly to hear what the missive contained.

'Lever asks particularly that I attend on Friday as he wishes to ask my advice on a military matter. Have you any notion what this might be?'

She nodded and her dark ringlets bobbed hard on either side of her face. 'I believe it is about his youngest son who has just come down from Oxford and wishes to enter the military. The boy wishes to join the cavalry but he and her ladyship are not sanguine about this.'

Toby sighed. 'The glory boys; he is more likely to be killed joining them. I shall speak to him, if by my intervention I can persuade him to make another choice then I suppose I must do it. Are you quite sure it is not to be a big occasion?'

'Indeed, Lady Lever was most insistent on that fact. I am so glad you have agreed to accompany us, it will do you good to mix in society after so long.' She reached out and patted his cheek as if she was his older sister. 'I shall send a reply directly, pray excuse me, Toby.'

'A minute more of your time, Celia. I met one Miss Victoria Marsh this morning, can you tell me anything about her?'

'She lives at Butterfield Hall, do you recall I pointed the building out to you when I accompanied you on your morning ride the other week?'

'I do, I was extremely uncivil to her, I wish to make my apologies. If I remember correctly it is a Mrs Winterton who owns the property?'

'It is. If Miss Marsh was abroad it must mean that Mrs Winterton has recovered from her illness. She is a delightful old lady and would be sorely missed if she passed on.'

Toby decided not to return to his bedchamber as he usually did, but to commandeer another mount and ride immediately to see Miss Marsh. He found the inane chitchat he encountered at social occasions tedious, so used his infirmity to avoid attending engagements. He would make an exception this Friday, with luck he could complete his business with Lord Lever and then secrete himself somewhere away from the other guests until it was time to depart.

The horse he'd ridden that morning was fit and quite able to go out again immediately. The Manor was secreted in a valley, a pretty grey stone building built a hundred years ago. He rode to the brow of the hill from where he could see across the countryside to the larger establishment that was his destination.

He stood in his stirrups, keeping his weight on his good leg, and stared into the distance; Butterfield Hall was a small shape almost hidden by the stand of substantial trees that surrounded it. The drive, a ribbon leading arrow-straight to the lane that wound its way through the fields and eventually joined the route he intended to take.

A movement on the drive attracted his attention. Yes, it was a gig and it appeared to have a female occupant. Could Miss Marsh be intending to call upon Celia? She was certainly heading in this direction. He scanned the countryside searching for a safe route across the fields. His mount was more than capable of jumping any obstacle in its path, however he was not sure he could remain in the saddle as his injured leg hung straight and he couldn't grip as he ought.

He was about to urge the gelding forward when a flash of metal caught the sunlight. He froze. He leaned forward narrowing his eyes to stare at the hedgerow that bordered the lane the girl would be travelling through very shortly. As he feared, there were two men behind the bushes, they were obviously waiting to ambush the unsuspecting girl. God knows why footpads should be targeting such a remote place, but he had no alternative. He must get to her before she came close enough to be in danger.

The only way he could achieve his objective was by taking the direct route, jumping the hedges and ditches that lay between him and the lane. He was unarmed so could not confront them, the only way to save Miss Marsh from a distressing experience was to reach her before she turned into the lane. Forgetting his fear of falling he kicked the horse into a gallop and hurtled headlong down the hill.

★　★　★

The gig was rattling along the lane at a spanking pace, Victoria was sanguine she would reach her destination in good time. Suddenly a massive horse landed not a few yards in front of them. Sam hauled on the reins in a desperate attempt to avoid a collision. Victoria was catapulted from the seat to land painfully on her knees in the well of the carriage. The horse that created the accident was riderless.

'Sam, some poor gentleman has taken a tumble, quickly now, go and investigate; he might need our assistance.' Whilst her driver scrambled down to do her bidding she gingerly pushed herself back on to the squabs. Before he reached the hedge the branches parted and she saw the mud streaked face of Major Highcliff. She straightened her bonnet, which had slipped forward over one eye, and glared at him.

'Have you run mad, sir? Your horse could have killed us.' He simply ignored her comment.

'I beg your pardon, but I had no alternative. You are in grave danger, you must return to your home immediately.'

The poor man it would appear had addled his wits when he had fallen. She smiled encouragingly at him. 'Remain where you are, Miss Marsh, I shall be with you directly I can find a way through this wretched hedge'

'Are you unhurt, sir? Do you need

my driver's assistance.'

He pokered up at her suggestion. 'I fell from my horse but, as you can see, I have not broken my neck. Here, my man, get that vehicle turned round, do not stand there gawping.'

Sam was holding the frightened horse. 'I'll not be able to turn round here, sir, I'll need to unharness the mare and do it by hand.'

Suddenly he emerged from a gap between the branches and all but fell headfirst into the ditch, before heaving himself out using his walking stick to assist him. He recovered his horse and using the wheel of the gig as a mounting block somehow rolled into the saddle.

'That will take too long. Miss Marsh, you must come up with me — your groom must ride his horse back as best he can. I saw two footpads waiting to waylay you, they could be here at any moment.'

It did not occur to her to argue, the major knew what he was about. She stood up and moved to the edge of the gig waiting for him to bring his horse closer. Without further ado he scooped her up and placed her in front of him. For some reason she felt quite safe within the circle of his arms; she did not care for large, spirited beasts but with him to hold her steady she knew she was in no danger.

Leaving Sam to follow, Major Highcliff urged his horse into a canter. She settled back into his embrace, her heart racing and her fingers clammy within her gloves. She knew who it had been in the lane. It was those two vagabonds waiting for her, somehow they had discovered her whereabouts and intended to steal back the valuable necklace she had in her possession.

How could they have known she would go to visit Sir John? There was only one logical explanation; they must have followed her back to Butterfield Hall. She closed her eyes, gritting her teeth to stop them chattering and an uncontrollable shivering overwhelmed her.

They had been watching the house hoping for an opportunity to take back the necklace, and have guessed she was on her way to The Manor to hand it in. It was unlikely such an efficient gang would not know that the local magistrate was Sir John Farnham. Her abode and his were the only two that had not yet been attacked.

'My dear girl, I shall soon have you safe. You have nothing to fear, relax against me, let me keep you warm.'

Unable to speak, she did as he suggested and he tucked his coat around her. The warmth from his body began to restore her and by the time they arrived her trembling had ceased.

'I am quite well, thank you, sir. If you will release me I can easily dismount unaided.'

He reined in and removed his jacket from her person. 'I shall take my horse around to the stables first, but then I need to speak to you.'

She slid to the ground and smiled up at him. 'And I must speak to you most urgently. I know who it was that wished to waylay me. I shall have refreshments brought to the drawing-room, ask a stable boy to direct you.'

★   ★   ★

Toby guided his exhausted horse through the archway and around to the cobbled yard. His leg hurt like the very devil, his hands were shaking like a blancmange and he would not be at all surprised if he'd damaged his shoulder in the crashing fall he'd taken. Before his injury he would have cleared that last hedge with no difficulty. The girl must think him a sorry specimen to be unable to stay in the saddle.

A groom hurried forward to take the sweating animal. 'Make sure he's walked until he's cool and then rub him down. I shall be some time here.'

There was the sound of hooves behind him and Miss Marsh's ancient groom appeared on the carriage horse. 'Your gig will come to no harm in the lane, far better to leave it than risk being shot by footpads.'

The man whistled through his teeth. 'Thank God you came along when you did, sir, I weren't armed and could not have put up a fight.'

Toby felt sufficiently recovered to risk dismounting. He hoped to accomplish this without pitching on to his nose; he needed to kick his feet from the stirrups and swing his right leg round. This manoeuvre required him to place himself face first across the saddle, then slide carefully to the ground making sure his good leg landed first.

He accomplished his clumsy dismount without embarrassment. Patting his horse he removed his walking stick. He carried it in the straps attached behind the saddle that would hold his rifle when on campaign. He turned to the three men watching him carefully, obviously believing they would need to offer their assistance. He grinned at them and nodded happily. 'Take good care of my horse, he has served me well today.'

He turned to the nearest stable lad and raised his eyebrow. The youth pulled his forelock and smiled back. 'Take the path the other side of the yard, sir, it will take you to the side door. It's far closer than going round to the front.'

It required all his fortitude to sway away without flinching. God knows what damage he'd done to his leg today, but it was worth it as his foolhardy ride had saved Miss Marsh from an unpleasant experience. Almost a hero, if only he'd managed to stay in the saddle for that final jump she would not have smiled at him as though he was in need of a bath chair.

Had he redeemed himself in her eyes by his behaviour following his tumble? Only time would tell if this enchanting young lady viewed him as a hopeless cripple or a man like any other.

His brow creased as he thought of her parting words. How the devil could she know who the footpads were? It was almost perplexing. He was obliged to pause outside the door before attempting to climb the two steps. He raised his hand to knock but it was opened by a smiling parlour maid who greeted him with due respect.

'Major Highcliff, Miss Marsh asks if you would care follow me to an anteroom where hot water is waiting for you. I shall conduct you to the drawing-room when you are done.' The girl curtsied and he swung inside, his cheeks flushed. He should be grateful that Miss Marsh had arranged for him to sort himself out downstairs, but it just emphasised his disability, he should have been conducted to a bedchamber.

He was shocked to discover how much mud there was on his person considering the ground was hard as a board. Ten minutes later the willing chambermaid had brushed his jacket for him, he had sponged his britches and washed his face and hands. He was now eager to join the courageous young woman who had participated in the extraordinary events without turning a hair. He'd never met another quite like her, if only he had met her last year before he had become such a sorry specimen.

Victoria had ample time to return to her chamber and remove her bonnet and spencer and get Beth to brush her skirts. She had sent a parlour maid to the kitchen to order them both much-needed sustenance. She had just returned to the drawing-room when she heard him approaching. Having missed her normal mid-day repast she was sharp set and she had not yet met a gentleman who wasn't ready to eat whatever was put before him. After his unfortunate experience he would no doubt wish to repair the damage to his appearance before joining her.

The door opened and Ellie bobbed. 'Major Highcliff to see you, Miss.'

'Thank you. Kindly leave the door open, Ellie, and ask Bennett to join us.' Far better to have the housekeeper sitting with them, than to risk her reputation. 'Come in, sir, and take a seat. I fear that if I don't sit down I shall collapse in a heap on the carpet.'

He bowed and his smile made her toes curl in her slippers. 'You have shown amazing fortitude, Miss Marsh, and I should think none the worse of you if you did give way to a fit of the vapours.'

She returned his smile and sank gratefully on to the small love seat. He immediately folded his length on to an upright chair on the far side of the carpet, his appearance fully restored and apparently suffering no ill effects from his parting company with his mount. He was obviously well aware of the possible impropriety of being closeted alone with her for he remained on edge until Bennett slipped in and sat unobtrusively in the alcove by the door. What she had to say to him would be better not spoken in front of a servant but an open door would not suffice to protect her good name.

The rattle of teacups heralded the arrival of the much desired refreshments. Two girls staggered in carrying a veritable feast; she had ordered Cook to send whatever there was in the kitchen, plus tea and coffee and fresh lemonade. She had no idea what a military gentleman preferred but hoped there would be something to his taste laid out on the two octagonal tables.

Toby waited until they were alone again before speaking, his voice soft so that they could not be heard. 'Miss Marsh, I wish to know what you meant by saying you knew who was waiting to attack you?'

She gestured towards the food, she could not possibly explain everything until she had eaten. 'I know this seems a vast amount, but I am extremely hungry. Excitement appears to have given me a prodigious appetite. If you don't mind, sir, I shall tell you everything when we have finished. Allow me to serve you. What would you like?' His compelling blue grey eyes widened slightly but he did not argue.

Instead he leant forward and examined the spread. 'Some of everything, if you please, and coffee to drink. Forgive me if I don't serve you, Miss Marsh. I fear I have rather overdone things, my leg is not completely healed, you know.'

Smiling, Victoria piled a plate with slices of succulent, home cured ham, fresh bread and butter, game pie and pickles. She placed it beside him on the small side table, along with his napkin and cutlery. Once she had served herself and they both had a steaming mug of the aromatic brew she preferred to tea, she grinned at him; he seemed far more approachable than he had been in the church that morning.

'Forgive me, Major Highcliff, if I eat my luncheon without further talk.'

'My sentiments exactly, Miss Marsh. Food first, discussion later.'

Replete, she pushed aside her plate and sighed. 'That's better. Do you mind if I enquire as to how you received your injury?'

He swallowed the last of his coffee and replaced the cup with a decided click in its saucer. Oh dear! Now she had offended him. To her surprise when he looked at her his expression was more sad than angry.

'My horse was shot from under me and fell, trapping my leg beneath it. I was lucky not to have lost it. I was more fortunate this morning.' She was mesmerised by his strange grey-blue eyes.

Her cheeks coloured under his scrutiny. 'I must thank you for your timely intervention, sir, it was most courageous considering your circumstances.'

The light in his eyes appeared to fade at her comment, she wondered what she had said to upset him. Bennett began to clear away the dirty crockery and cutlery and, obviously forgetting she was supposed to remain in the room with them, vanished carrying one of the trays.

As she returned to her seat her eye was drawn to her reticule discarded as if it contained no more than the usual feminine fall-lalls. It was high time to tell the major what she had seen earlier and hand the necklace over to him for safe keeping, also to explain why the footpads had been hoping to waylay her. Picking up the bag she carried it to her place.

'Something happened this morning when I was walking to Bentley that I believe could have a bearing on what has just taken place.' She removed the jewel and held it up for his inspection. His eyes widened and he looked suitably impressed.

'That is reason indeed, Miss Marsh. Those men must be desperate to recover the necklace — it's worth a king's ransom.'

Briefly she explained what had taken place on her walk to the village. 'Major, my aunt has been desperately ill, she is already very agitated about these local burglaries and expects that we will be targeted next. If she discovers what happened today it might well prove fatal to her.'

'I understand. I fear that I must agree

with Mrs Winterton, this establishment is ripe for the picking. But do not look so worried, my dear, I shall not let harm come to you, I give you my word.' He held out his hand. 'Toss the item to me, if you please.'

She did as he bid. The sunlight caught the diamonds as they spiralled through the air. Surely this was not the way to treat such a precious piece of jewellery? He examined it more closely.

'I shall take care of this until it can be returned to its rightful owners.' He tucked it into his jacket pocket and stood up. 'Forgive me, Miss Marsh, I must take my leave. I thank you for the repast and hope that you will not suffer nightmares because of your experience.'

'And I thank you, sir, for coming so nobly to my rescue. It is a coincidence indeed that we should meet again so soon after this morning's chance encounter.'

His cheeks flushed and he nodded, a rueful smile curving his lips. 'Actually, my dear, I was coming to see you in order to apologise for my rudeness this morning. Am I forgiven?'

She dipped in a low curtsey to hide her blushes. 'I have forgotten it already, Major Highcliff.'

'I shall arrange for some of Sir John's men to scour the woods and surrounding area for those villains, they will not be allowed to remain in this vicinity. You may sleep without fear of robbery tonight.'

Ellie, the parlour maid, appeared to conduct him from the house. The room seemed strangely empty after he'd gone. Victoria hurried to the window to observe him cantering away down the drive. She has just turned away when her aunt arrived looking better than she had for weeks.

'My love, you will never guess, we have been invited to an informal party at Buckfast Abbey, the house of the new Lord and Lady Lever. Is that not exciting?'

3

'I did not know that we were on visiting terms with such illustrious neighbours, Aunt Martha.'

'My dear girl, neither did I. The previous Lord Lever was a recluse, never came into society at all. It must be that the year of mourning is now up and they can start entertaining again. Remember, my dear, your uncle was a respectable man and very deep in the pocket and I believe that we are an important family in the neighbour-hood.'

'We are on good terms with Sir John and Lady Farnham, I suppose, so why should they not include us in their first soiree?'

Thrilled with the thought of attend-ing such a prestigious event it was some time before the conversation turned to the visit of the major. 'My dear, what's this I hear about you having a gentleman caller?' Her aunt smiled knowingly and patted her hand.

Good grief! How quickly the information had travelled upstairs. If the major had still been with her she would have been obliged to introduce him to Aunt Martha. 'Major Highcliff, Sir John's brother-in-law, came to my assistance . . . he has been staying with them whilst he was recovering from a serious injury to his leg. I met him at the church this morning, that is how I knew who he was.'

Her aunt viewed her with alarm. 'But it does not explain what you were doing that required his assistance.'

'Remember, Aunt Martha, I was to visit Sir John to ask for his advice. It was on my way that Major Highcliff arrived to tell me he'd seen a pair of footpads waiting to waylay me. Naturally he escorted me home.' She thought it better not to mention he'd fallen from his horse, he was obviously embarrassed enough about this incident. It was remarkable that he'd managed to stay put for as long as he did; in her opinion only a very brave man would even have attempted such a ride when all he had to keep him in the saddle was his sense of balance.

Better not to say she'd ridden with him or that Sam had left the gig somewhere in the lane to be collected later. It was also wisest not to further distress her ancient relative by telling her about the necklace. Outdoor news rarely filtered through to the inside staff, which was fortuitous in the circumstances. 'Indeed, Major Highcliff promised the area would be thoroughly searched and any remaining footpads flushed out. That means we can sleep safely in our beds knowing we will not be a target for a burglary tonight.'

'That is a relief. What manner of man is this major? You spent a prodigiously long time with him, and Bennett informs me that between you, you devoured enough to feed a small army.'

Victoria's laugh filled the room. 'He is an extremely tall man, with dark hair and blue-grey eyes. Although he can be charming, he is of uncertain temper, little patience and inclined to be dictatorial.'

Her dry answer appeared to please. 'I see that you were taken with him, no doubt you will meet again on Friday night. I should be interested to see this gentleman who has succeeded where none other have.'

'Aunt Martha, you are incorrigible. I can assure you that Major Highcliff does not interest me in that way. He must be in his thirties, far too old for me. And the last person I would choose as a partner would be a military gentleman, for they would be for ever ordering me about as if I were one of their soldiers.'

★   ★   ★

The following morning Victoria was in her sitting-room attempting to complete a watercolour of the park when a familiar figure turned in through the gates and cantered up the drive. She was forced to admit that despite his infirmity the major was an excellent horseman, it was impossible to tell he only had the use of one leg.

It was a little after 11 o'clock, not the accepted time for a morning call, these should not start until after luncheon. Her lips twitched, one could hardly expect a gentleman like him to be aware of such niceties. She must check that her hair was still tidy and that she had no paint on her person. Removing the apron she wore to protect her gown she returned to her bedchamber where Beth, her maid, was changing the bed linen.

'Have I any paint on me, Beth?'

The girl smiled and shook her head. 'You look as pretty as a picture, Miss Marsh, and no smudges anywhere.'

Victoria glanced down at her dress, pleased that she had chosen to wear something so becoming as her new eau de nil, sprigged muslin. Should she wait in her parlour or be downstairs in the drawing-room working on her needle-point? She hesitated, then shook her head. Whatever next! She had received dozens of gentlemen callers over the past three years and never been in such a fluster before. It must be because Major Highcliff was a man of maturity, not a green boy like the others that had visited.

She would go down, and if she met him in the entrance hall then so be it. She would not allow this formidable visitor to unsettle her further or her aunt would draw the wrong conclusions and be hinting of a match before the day was out. Halfway along the passage she heard a crash and a cry of pain. It had come from her aunt's apartment.

Her heart pounding she gathered up her skirts and burst into the parlour to find not Aunt Martha, but Mary, a chambermaid spread-eagled on the boards. It was obvious the girl had been balancing on a chair in order to dust the ceiling and had managed to tumble from it.

'Mary, stay where you are, let me check that you have broken no limbs before you attempt to rise.'

'Lawks a mussy! I'm ever so sorry, miss, I was so distracted looking out the window and missed my footing. I reckon I've turned my ankle, it don't half hurt a bit.'

Victoria knew what had attracted the girl's attention, it had been the arrival of Major Highcliff. That man seemed to bring disaster in his wake. 'I believe that your ankle is sprained, let me assist you to the chair, I shall ring for help. Cook can put a cold compress on for you, and you must sit with it up for a day or two. No doubt Bennett can find you something to occupy your time until you are fit enough to resume your normal duties.'

By the time she had dealt with the poor girl almost 20 minutes had passed. Aunt Martha and the major would think her decidedly impolite for not appearing sooner. As she left the room she caught a glimpse of herself in the

45

mirror. Her eyes widened, she had several curls escaping from her arrangement and far worse, the hem of her dress was liberally coated with dust and cobwebs.

She could not appear like this, she must return to her rooms and repair the damage. Unfortunately as she stepped out into the passageway she came face-to-face with an agitated Bennett. 'Miss Marsh, you must come at once, the mistress is getting worked up and you know the doctors said she must remain calm at all times.'

As the housekeeper appeared not to notice her dishevelment, Victoria decided she had no option but to hurry downstairs and make her apologies. On the way she did her best to brush off the dirt, there was nothing she could do about her hair. She paused to catch her breath before sailing into the drawing-room.

Aunt Martha's shocked expression told her she had made the wrong decision — she should have changed her gown.

Major Highcliff pushed himself upright and nodded, it was amusement she could see in his eyes, not censure. Reassured by his reaction she curtsied and smiled with more warmth than was called for. His expression changed, his eyes blazed as if you wish to devour her.

'Good morning, Major Highcliff, I do apologise for keeping you waiting. I had to deal with a small domestic emergency.' He waited politely until she was settled next to her aunt and then resumed his place.

'Miss Marsh, I have just been telling Mrs Winterton the good news. Sir John and I led a substantial group of men in a second thorough search of the neighbourhood. Those footpads are no longer in the vicinity.'

'That is certainly welcome news, sir. I am sure that everyone is much relieved that the persecution from these burglars is at an end.' There was no sign of any refreshments, he had obviously come merely to deliver his message. If that was the case, then why had he remained until she eventually appeared?

'Victoria, my dear, I have invited the major to join us for luncheon and he has kindly accepted. It is now past noon, and Bennett is waiting to serve.'

'Then let us prepare to the small dining-room, I believe we are to have leak and potato potage, it is a great favourite of mine.' She smiled at their guest. 'Are you attending the soiree at the Lever's on Friday?'

He offered his arm to her aunt before answering. 'I have been invited, Miss Marsh.'

She scowled at his departing back. Did she think she was hanging out for an offer? He must have a very high opinion of his worth if that was the case. Aunt Martha was chattering away quite happily, he did not depress her pretensions or look down his nose at her. Perhaps he thought a penniless young woman of barely 20 years beneath his notice, no doubt he would fraternise with the upper echelons of their small society.

Over luncheon her aunt encouraged him to tell lively anecdotes about his experiences on the Peninsular. Before the meal was completed she had found herself drawn to his wit and intelligence, and the fact that he was without doubt the most handsome man of her acquaintance added to his charm. If only he could always be so pleasant she might be prepared to like him a little better.

He took his leave promptly, bowed politely to Aunt Martha and nodded to her. He had scarcely quit the room before her aunt began.

'It is most unfortunate that you chose to come down in disarray, Victoria, he must have thought you do not care about your appearance.' Her aunt shook her head in reproof. 'It would not do to give him the wrong impression, he is such a charming and handsome gentleman. I believe he is exactly right for you.'

'If I had returned to my chambers to change I would have been even later, and Major Highcliff's opinion is of no import to me. He is undoubtedly an amusing and eloquent gentleman but not at all my style. He is far too old for one thing, in my limited experience I have noticed that older gentlemen tend to treat their wives like children. That would not do for me, I can heartily assure you.'

She smiled at her aunt and patted her shoulder before exiting the drawing-room. She would take a brisk walk around the park to mull over what had transpired. For all her protestations there was something about the major that drew her to him. Although he had paid her no particular interest, why had he agreed to share a meal with them? It could not have been for Aunt Martha's company, so she must conclude it was for hers.

During her promenade she came to a decision, she must nip this fanciful notion of Aunt Martha's in the bud. On Friday she would make sure she paid attention to any other gentleman but him, make it clear to anyone present and she was not hanging out for a husband. However sensible this was, she could not help but feel regret that she would not now be getting to know the major better.

Matrimony was a laudable aim for all young ladies, but she had no intention of leaving her aunt to embark on this happy state. One day she would fall in love, but until that happened she would not allow herself to be interested in a particular gentleman even, if his smile made her heart beat a little bit faster.

4

'You look stunning, my dear, the emerald green was an inspired choice. I must own I wasn't sure when you selected the material, but now I see it made up I must agree with you.'

'Thank you, Aunt Martha, as the invitation stated tonight was not to be a formal occasion, I am not sure that I have made the right choice. I have no wish to look overdressed.'

Her aunt shook her head the vehemently. 'No, it is perfect for the occasion. The neck line is rather low — you know I hate to see any young ladies with a plunging decolletage.'

Victoria busied herself with the ribbon that held the demi-train secure over her wrist, while she considered her reply. 'It's far too late to change into something else, I believe I heard the carriage outside.'

'If you are not the most beautiful young woman present, I shall eat my best bonnet. Come along, we must not be tardy.' The egret feathers on her magnificent burgundy turban danced and the heavy silk crackled as her aunt sailed downstairs and out to the waiting barouche. The weather was so clement they had decided it would be far more pleasant to travel in an open carriage this evening.

The drive was short, it hardly gave her time to compose herself, she was not sure if she was eager to further her acquaintance with the formidable major, or whether she was going to follow her plan to make it clear she was not interested in him in any way. Her aunt was her usual garrulous self and fortunately did not notice Victoria's absentminded replies. As they neared their destination Sam, resplendent in full livery, was obliged to join a substantial queue of similar carriages all heading in the same direction.

'Goodness me, my dear, it would

seem this event is far from the small soirée we were expecting.' Her aunt sounded positively delighted that there were to be more than one hundred guests instead of the expected dozen or so. Victoria was not so sanguine, she was not used to mixing in society and had never before attended an evenings entertainment with so many guests.

Eventually it was their turn and Sam drew up expertly at the bottom of the steps. It was strange to be descending from the carriage in full evening dress at five o'clock in the afternoon on a glorious summer's day. Two gardeners pushing wheelbarrows had stopped to stare, they did not seem overly impressed by the show of wealth and luxury displayed before them.

A fully uniformed footman let down the steps, a second was waiting to assist them from the carriage. The august gentleman standing at the door must be the butler. He bowed them in.

Whereupon they joined the others threading their way through the vast black and white tiled entrance hall, past the imposing staircase and eventually to be greeted by Lord and Lady Lever.

'At last, Mrs Winterton and Miss Marsh are here, my dear.' His lordship beamed at Victoria. His wife, ignoring convention, stepped forward to embrace her.

'Miss Marsh, I cannot tell you how grateful I am that you found my precious necklace. It is a family heirloom you know, has been handed down through generations to the eldest daughter in the family. I should have been devastated if it had not been returned to me.'

'It was my pleasure, my lady.'

'Now, Miss Marsh, allow me to introduce you to my daughters. This is Emily, this Charlotte, I hope that they will both become dear friends of yours now that you have met.'

Victoria curtsied to Emily, who looked as if she was about her own age. 'I am delighted to meet you. What a lovely gown you have on, it suits your fair complexion perfectly.'

This was exactly the right thing to say as the girls' slightly supercilious expression changed instantly to a delighted smile. 'I know, Mama says flounces and bows are all the rage in London.' Victoria hid her smile behind her fan, there were so many ruffles and furbelows on Emily's ensemble it was a wonder the girl could walk.

Charlotte remained silent but her eyebrows raised a fraction, Victoria liked her instantly. A young man at the end of the line stepped forward.

'I say, is no one going to introduce Miss Marsh to me?'

His doting mama smiled up at him. 'Miss Marsh, allow me to present to you our youngest son, it is on his behalf that we have persuaded Major Highcliff to attend our small get-together.'

He bowed extravagantly and she curtsied. He was a handsome young man with a shock of corn coloured hair and the merriest brown eyes she'd ever seen. The press of people prevented further conversation and she and her aunt moved on into the ballroom. Her eyes rounded. If this was Lady Lever's idea of a small get-together she shuddered to think what a grand occasion might be like.

'My dear, I shall join my friends at the far side of the ballroom — you see that group of chairs? I can watch you dance from there. Now, go and enjoy yourself. See, already there are several young gentleman looking your way.'

Victoria was well aware that she had become a focal point for unwanted attention. The last thing she required was to be cast adrift amongst these predatory gentlemen. Before she could protest, however, her aunt forged through the crowd like a small burgundy ship in full sail and she was alone.

Frantically she glanced around; how long until the dancing started when most of the gentleman would be with partners on the polished boards? She must absent herself at once. Too late

— she was surrounded. She could neither back away nor move forward for fear of touching one of the crowd. To her astonishment the foremost were suddenly thrust aside and she found herself face-to-face with the major. Magnificent in his regimentals, the scarlet jacket and gold frogging emphasising his good looks.

'Excuse me, gentlemen, you are de trop. Miss Marsh, allow me to escort you to somewhere less busy.'

She willingly placed her hand on his arm, she was shocked to find the muscles rigid, she glanced nervously up to him. He smiled widely but it did not reach his eyes. He was angry, she prayed it was not her that had infuriated him. He marched her through the milling throng in the ballroom and out on to the terrace where others were strolling, enjoying the early evening sunshine away from the overcrowded interior. Where was his cane? Would he fall without its support?

'Miss Marsh, what were you thinking?

To stand so publicly in the centre of the room with no companion or chaperone? It was the height of folly.'

She removed her arm and glided gracefully to the stone balustrade. 'Major Highcliff, I thank you for your intervention, it was most timely and much appreciated.' It would have been wiser to have left it there, but something prompted her to continue. 'However, sir, how I disport myself is no concern of yours. I was unaware that I had become your responsibility.'

His eyes narrowed and he stared down at her. 'As you have no male relative to protect your reputation, I thought it behoved me to step in. Was I wrong in thinking you distressed? Did you not wish me to rescue you from that circle of buffoons?'

'Of course I did. Did I not just thank you for it? A gentleman would have escorted me to safety without feeling the need to censure me in that unpleasant way.' He was impossible. Why did he persist in treating her like a naughty schoolgirl?

He ignored her comments. 'Do you wish to become a focal point for unpleasant gossip in this neighbourhood?'

With difficulty she restrained the urge to stamp her foot. 'No, I don't.' She glared up at him. 'But your behaviour, sir, is attracting far more attention than anything I might have done.'

A flicker of amusement lightened his expression. 'Touché, my dear. You are right to castigate me.'

He stepped closer to her, to an observer would appear he was merely discussing the attractive view over the gardens, she knew better. The hardness of his thigh pressed against hers and a strange warmth engulfed her. Was she succumbing to a summer cold? Her pulse was agitated, she had never experienced anything quite like this.

His voice was soft, caressing almost. 'I shall say no more, Miss Marsh, but be sure I shall be watching you tonight.

Behave with decorum.'

Then he was gone leaving her to make sense of what had passed between them. It was the outside of enough that the virtual stranger should address her in such a way, it was as if he had some right . . . her heart skipped a beat. She spun to see he was leaning nonchalantly against the wall staring in her direction. He smiled and her annoyance melted. She had not mistaken the matter. He intended to pursue her for himself, believing that already he had the right of a future husband to dictate her actions.

Never! She would not tie herself to him, he would wish to take control of her life, she would have no freedom at all. Ignoring the fact that he was the first man to make her heart race, that since she had met him last week there had not been a moment in the day when she had not thought of him, she decided to put into action the plan she had formulated. After tonight Major Highcliff would be in no doubt that his interest was not reciprocated.

* ⋆ ⋆ ⋆

Toby watched her expression change from annoyance, to alarm and finally to determination. Dash it! He should not have interfered, should have left her to cope with the circle of importunate young gentlemen all vying to attract her attention. Her vulnerability, her innocence, had awakened something within him and before he had time to reconsider, he was at her side and routing her adversaries.

Then first he had aggravated matters by chiding her as if she were a child and not a beautiful young woman, and then given her a quite erroneous impression that he was pursuing her himself. Her reaction to this had been instant, she was not best pleased. His sudden laugh turned several heads in his direction as if he were deranged. She had thrown down a challenge, it was irresistible. He would show this headstrong young woman that he was a redoubtable adversary.

His blood pulsed round his body in a

way it had not done since his accident. Could it be that he was regaining his spirits because of her? His head was spinning at the implication, he needed to be alone, he could not remain amongst all this noise and bustle. Without thinking, he vaulted over the balustrade and landed in the soft dirt of the flower border, his injured leg buckled and he almost pitched on to his nose. Cursing his stupidity he leant against the wall until the pain subsided.

He cursed volubly, why, just when he was beginning to feel like a useful man again did his body let him down? Even though his spirits were improved, his leg would never recover. What was the point in pursuing Miss Marsh? She would not wish to ally herself with someone like him. The thought of her seeing his hideous scars made his stomach clench in horror.

He would hobble around to the stables to locate John's carriage and retrieve his cane. Although he would far prefer to return to the privacy of The

Manor, something held him back, he could not leave Miss Marsh unprotected. He must trust to her not to do anything rash in his absence.

★ ★ ★

Victoria removed her empty dance card from her reticule and set off determined to have it filled before the major came to interfere. She entered the ballroom and immediately was waylaid by Mr Lever.

'Miss Marsh, I have been searching for you everywhere. I wish to lead you out in the opening set and it is forming now.'

Her face was radiant. 'Thank you, sir, I'd be honoured to partner you.'

He guided her to the head of the group, he bowed and she curtsied and took her place opposite him. Then the music started and she was so busy concentrating on the intricacies of the dance she had little time for conversation, barely heard what he said to her, merely nodded and smiled when she thought it appropriate. When the final chords died away she was quite breathless. She curtsied, he bowed.

'I must write in your card, Miss Marsh, that I am to have the supper dance. It would not do for any other fellow to scribble his name in my place.' Silently she handed it over and watched him scrawl his name for the first two sets and the supper dance. He glanced at her with a mischievous smile. 'Do you think anyone would notice if I claim a third dance?'

'Indeed, you must not. Please return my card at once, the music is about to recommence.'

When he escorted her back to the edge of the ballroom she was immediately surrounded by eager young gentlemen wishing to add their names to her card. This was not how it should be, she was fairly sure a young lady should not agreed to partner a gentleman to whom she had not been introduced.

'Enough, I do not appreciate being jostled in this way. If you wish to dance with me then you must find someone to effect an introduction first. Pray excuse me, I have business elsewhere.'

She left the group gawping after her in surprise. Where was Aunt Martha? She would go and sit with her until a suitable gentleman was introduced to her. She had barely settled herself on the small wooden chair when Lady Lever arrived.

'Miss Marsh, I have here several gentleman who are most insistent that I introduce them.'

As each of the young men were named she was obliged to hand over her dance card. Within a short space of time every slot was filled, but she was not to partner anyone twice apart from Mr Lever. She shrugged helplessly at her aunt as she was led away by a Mr Giles Sanderson. He was as eager as a puppy and she could not help laughing at his antics.

When Mr Lever appeared to claim

her for his second dance she greeted him with more enthusiasm than she'd intended, but he seemed like an old friend after the constant stream of unknown gentlemen she had been obliged to partner. She was almost certain at least three of them had promised to call the following day to pay their respects. They were all so immature, talked of nothing but hunting and shooting, and didn't listen to a word she said in return.

'Miss Marsh, you look a trifle flushed, would you prefer to take a turn on the terrace before we go in to supper?'

Without hesitation she agreed. 'There is nothing I would like more, sir, I am quite fatigued after all the sets I have been obliged to stand up in.' Outside it was now almost dark, she drew in a cool breath of clean, fresh air. She sighed, it was a perfect summer's evening, the last blackbirds singing as they settled for the night. She was unaware that he had led her into the shadows of an alcove at the far end of the terrace. 'It has been a most enjoyable evening, I cannot remember having had such fun.'

'I am glad to hear you say so, Miss Marsh. You remember that I told you I am to join a cavalry regiment, do you prefer a man in uniform?'

Unbidden an image of the major filled her thoughts and her lips curved. Before she could protest the young man had grasped her upper arms and was dragging her into his embrace. Outraged she lashed out with her feet but her evening slippers made no impression on his shins.

'Unhand me, sir, you are no gentleman to treat me with such disrespect.' He was no longer the smiling youth she'd imagined, his eyes were dark, his expression determined. He was far stronger than she had ever imagined. If she screamed she would be saved but at what cost to her reputation? No respectable young lady would have agreed to accompany a gentleman into the shadows. His weight was pressing her into the wall, the rough stones painful through her thin evening gown.

Then she was free, Mr Lever disappeared headfirst into the flower bed below the terrace and the major was beside her.

'Miss Marsh, you have less sense than a pea goose. Whatever possessed you to come outside with that jackanapes?' His tone was brisk, she could not have borne it if he had been sympathetic. What must he think of her? She could not bring herself look at him.

'Come, my dear, I shall escort you to your carriage. I had come to tell you that Mrs Winterton wishes to leave, she is finding the noise and press of people too much for her delicate state of health.'

Somehow she was sitting beside Aunt Martha in their carriage in the concealing darkness and she had not had the grace to thank him for his timely intervention. How could she have thought him anything but a gentleman?

She turned her face against the window glad that her aunt had drifted asleep and could not hear her crying; he must think her no better than a common flirt and she did so wish him to think well of her.

5

The following afternoon there was a constant stream of callers, but the only one she wished to see was conspicuous by his absence. Victoria retired to her bed chamber early with a migraine, it was a suitable punishment for her disgraceful behaviour the previous night. She had had her comeuppance, and it if it hadn't been for the major her reputation would be in tatters. If he didn't appear the next day she would write him a note of apology and ask him to call.

The sound of Beth in the dressing-room woke her the next day. Her head was still sore but she felt quite well enough to rise. She would walk to Bentley and visit with Marybeth, her friend had been unable to attend the party as she was confined to her chambers with a heavy cold.

'Aunt Martha, I am going to visit the vicarage. Do you require anything from the village shop?'

'No, my dear, you run along you look decidedly washed out this morning. Are you expecting any further gentlemen callers this afternoon?'

Victoria shuddered. 'I hope not, I have no time for such nonsense.'

She had got no further than the stile that led into the home meadow before realising she could not continue, the bright sunlight was aggravating her headache. She must return, remain indoors until it passed completely.

*   *   *

Toby knew he was in trouble when his eyes began to blur a mile or so from his destination. He must press on regardless, what he had just learned meant that Miss Marsh and her aunt were in grave danger. It was up to him to protect them, John was in Town, there was no one else. It was many months since he had been struck down in this way, what a cursedly awkward moment for his ague to reappear. He thundered into the stable yard scattering buckets and boys in all directions, fortunately his mount had the sense to stop before smashing into the wall.

Somehow he rolled from the saddle, but his legs gave way and he staggered as he reached the ground. He must remain conscious until he had warned them. The flagstones were pleasantly cool on his burning face. Footsteps were approaching rapidly.

'You feeling bad, major? I reckon you've overdone it gallivanting all over the countryside.'

He recognised the voice as that of Sam, the head groom. 'Here, Tom, give us a hand here, we need to get the major inside. He certainly ain't going nowhere today.'

Hands hooked themselves under his arms and he was hoisted unceremoniously to his feet. 'I shall be recovered presently, give me a moment and then I shall be able to continue. I . . . '

'No, sir, you ain't well enough to walk without our help. I reckons as you would be better stopping here tonight until you feel more the thing. Lean on us and we will get you inside safely enough.'

Toby needed the two men's assistance to negotiate what had become a gruelling distance from the stable to the side door. Sweat was trickling freely down his face by the time he'd achieved his objective and he could no longer remember why he'd ridden here in such a foolhardy fashion.

He scarcely remembered his passage through the house, it took all his concentration and fortitude to negotiate the interminable staircase. It was with considerable relief that he felt himself dropped gently on to the bed. Someone stripped him and then he was between cool sheets and was being offered a refreshing drink of lemonade.

★ ★ ★

The sound of running feet interrupted Victoria as she was explaining to her aunt why she had returned.

Ellie appeared in the doorway. 'Madam, Major Highcliff has arrived but the poor gentleman has collapsed in the stable yard. Sam and Tom are carrying him in, what shall they do with him?'

Victoria was on her feet, her stomach clenched in horror. 'I shall deal with this, Aunt Martha, I feared this might happen one day, he has been overdoing it dreadfully.'

'Take him to the best chamber, Victoria, I shall send Sam for the doctor.'

'I think it would be wiser to send for Sir John, he will know what to do for the best.' Victoria turned to the maid. 'I shall come with you, Ellie, we must take off the holland covers and make sure that the bed is not damp. It is some time since it was used.'

There was no time to worry about why the major had come so urgently and she must forget the unfortunate incident that had taken place at the Lever's supper party. He looked to be desperately ill, his face was deathly white and he appeared not to be aware of his surroundings. Certainly her aunt, who viewed him as he was carried past, shook her head sadly. Within a short while their unexpected guest was comfortably established and a message was on its way to Sir John.

Victoria was waiting to speak to the housekeeper, who had been attending to the patient. She hovered in the doorway of the drawing-room looking most anxious.

'Madam, Miss Marsh, Major Highcliff is seriously ill. I believe him to have a bout of the sweating fever; it's well known that this malady can reappear unexpectedly, especially if the person concerned has overtaxed himself.'

'How dreadful! I shall come at once to take care of him. He should never have galloped pell-mell across country.' She was already on her feet; she would brook no argument on this matter.

'Victoria, my dear girl, it is quite inappropriate for you to enter a gentleman's bedchamber. You must leave the nursing to Bennett, we have sent word to Sir John. No doubt he will send someone to look after the major directly he receives the message.'

'I'm sorry, Aunt Martha; remember, I am an expert in the sickroom having nursed you and both my parents through their final illnesses. Bennett can remain in the room at all times. I could not live with myself if our unexpected guest suffered permanent damage to his health when I could have done something to prevent it.'

Leaving her great aunt bewailing her impetuosity to Jenny, her abigail, she hurried into the hall, the housekeeper close behind. 'Bennett, I shall need a jug of tepid water, some clean cloths and another jug of freshly made lemonade. It is imperative that I reduce the fever and ensure that Major Highcliff takes plenty of fluids to replace that which he will lose through the sweating.'

What Bennett thought of her demands she had no idea and cared less. She would do her duty, and if her actions made him more comfortable then perhaps she had, in some way, repaid him for his timely intervention when she had been accosted by Mr Lever.

She was shocked to find the major pale and wan, perspiration trickling down his face, his eyes closed and his lips moving as if in prayer. The first thing was to get a cooling breeze into the chamber. 'Bennett, open the windows, this room is far too hot.'

She could hear the housekeeper muttering under her breath at such an unusual request.

Quickly soaking a cloth in the water she began to bathe his forehead, his shoulders and arms. She did not dare push the sheet down further, or enquire if Sam had left the patient's undergarment in place. She was already breaking every rule by being here; to be touching the unclothed limbs of a gentleman to whom she was not wed would mean instant ruin if ever it became known in public.

So be it. What was a reputation when her intervention could save his life? She wrung out the cloth and began her work again, pausing momentarily to spoon lemonade between his hot, dry lips.

As soon as someone arrived from The Manor she would hand over the nursing to them. What could possibly have made him thunder across country in that way, putting his own health at risk?

An hour or so later his fever was abating, his skin much cooler to the touch, the hectic flush on his cheek-bones all but gone. He lay, his top half exposed and although she knew it was most immodest she could not help but notice the breadth of his shoulders, the black hair that curled down the centre of his chest. There were several faint, white lines crisscrossing his naked torso, he had obviously been wounded several times before the near fatal accident that had brought him to Bentley to recuperate.

His eyes flickered open and he seemed to recognise her, his lips curved and then he fell deeply asleep. The tension eased from between her shoulders, her unorthodox treatment had been successful, he was out of danger and would no doubt be sitting up demanding his supper in a few hours. Should she wake him from his slumber and ask why he had ridden here at such a pace? Heaven knows what damage he had done. Thoughtfully she pulled the sheet up to his chin and turned to Bennett.

'I can leave him in your capable hands now, it might well be advisable for me not to be in the chamber when Sir John arrives.'

The housekeeper nodded. 'No one shall ever know you have been in here, it will remain a secret between us. It's nothing short of a miracle how you have reduced his fever, I shall remember to do the same if any of the staff are ever similarly stricken.'

Victoria returned to the drawing-room where Aunt Martha greeted her with some relief. 'Bennett is taking care of our patient, he is making good progress so she tells me.'

'Good girl, I am glad that you have listened to my advice. It should not be long before someone arrives from The Manor.'

However it was a while later before the sound of a carriage on the gravel alerted them. They both stood up and waited expectantly but Ellie appeared closely followed by an older man. 'Madam, Sir John is away from home, but the major's man, Digby, has come to take care of him.'

Victoria turned to her aunt indicating that she would take the valet upstairs. She explained to him what she had done to improve the major's condition. 'I have brought his fever down by sponging him with tepid water, he is now sleeping comfortably. I believe that it is imperative he takes fluids frequently, you must wake him to spoon the liquid in.'

'I have not been obliged to take care of him when he is so stricken, I reckon your treatment makes sense, Miss Marsh. I shall certainly continue to follow your instructions.' He grinned and added. 'If you don't mind me asking, miss, where did you get this idea from?'

'My father suffered frequently from the ague which he picked up when he was travelling in India. I do know of what I speak. In the absence of Jew's bark, which is most efficacious in treating this malady, the treatment produces a rapid reduction in fever.'

The valet nodded and slid past her to rest his hand on the major's forehead. 'He's a lot cooler and more comfortable than I expected him to be, Miss Marsh.'

'Digby, do you have any idea why the major came here in such a hurry? He was unable to tell us before he collapsed into unconsciousness.'

'No, miss, I don't. But he was concerned about something he had overheard in the village. When he left The Manor this morning he took his pistols with him.'

A shiver slid down her spine. Had he been coming to warn her of some impending danger?

'When the major wakes and is able to tell you anything, kindly send word to me in the drawing-room at once.'

It was decidedly unsettling to have the major on his sick bed and know that two loaded pistols had accompanied him. She had better not discuss this with her aunt, it would not do to upset her. No doubt the major had sent word to Sir John asking him to return, but in case he had not done, she would send a groom to The Manor . . . how silly she was. Her wits were wandering, of course a message would already have been sent to Town to inform Sir John and Lady Farnham that Major Highcliff was taken ill.

A wave of relief washed over her. She recalled that Lady Farnham had told her she was going to London to visit her mantua maker, it was barely a three hour journey to the metropolis. This meant Sir John might well be back before it got full dark, before there was any risk of robbers breaking in. It could only be this that had brought the major to their door so precipitously, the gang of thieves must have returned to the neighbourhood to continue their nefarious activities.

She almost missed her footing and tumbled headlong down the stairs when another, far more worrying, thought occurred to her. From all reports there were several ruffians involved, with Sir John and Lady Farnham absent from home, would they take this opportunity to burgle The Manor as well? Good grief! The children would still be in residence, she must do something. Ten minutes later the note was written and Tom on his way to deliver it. She had not told him the contents, just that it was imperative someone in authority should read it immediately.

Her aunt decided to retire early saying that too much excitement in one day was fatiguing. There had been no sign of Sir John and it would be dark in another couple of hours. Victoria had spoken to the housekeeper and asked her to be most punctilious in locking up the house that night as she had reason to believe the thieves were back in the neighbourhood. Bennett had said that tonight she would draw the inside shutters and fasten them securely, something not usually done during the summer months.

Victoria dared not tell her aunt she fully expected the brigands to break in that very night. She kissed her fondly and escorted her to the drawing-room door where Jenny was waiting. 'Good-night, make sure you take your sleeping draught, the doctor was most insistent about this. You need a good night's sleep.'

Tonight it was imperative that her aunt did not wake. The thought that the major was incapacitated filled her with dismay. The weapons he'd brought with him must be in his bedchamber. When everyone was asleep she would go to speak to Digby, take over as nurse whilst he stood guard.

Her mind was whirling with possibilities, she must clear her head before she embarked on her next inappropriate action. It was a fine night, it could to no harm to take a quick walk around the garden. If she kept within a one hundred yards of the house she should be in no danger. It was possible there were intruders in the woods waiting for their opportunity to break in, but as far as she knew they had never caused anyone physical harm, therefore it was unlikely she would be attacked. It was valuables they were after, and they were unlikely to take lives.

6

Toby opened his eyes to find himself in a chamber he did not recognise. Where the devil was he? He felt slightly light headed and lethargic — he must have collapsed from a bout of his recurring fever. Something was gnawing at him, something he had to do, but his mind refused to grasp what it was.

He closed his eyes, relaxed, letting thoughts drift hoping his memory would return. He remembered soft, feminine hands sponging him down, spooning liquid into his mouth. Good grief! He must be at Butterfield Hall, it could have been none other than Miss Marsh who had taken care of him in this most intimate of fashions.

Why had he come here? He could recall galloping flat out across the fields but nothing else. Where were his garments? He must get up at once.

There was someone moving around next door. He looked sideways but could see no brass bell to ring. He must get himself out of bed and ask whoever it was for their assistance in finding his clothes.

He was just about upright when Digby emerged from the dressing room. 'Major Highcliff, sir, I beg you return to your bed. Two hours ago you were barely conscious, it cannot be good for you to be out of bed so soon.'

Toby ignored the comment. 'Help me to dress, I have something important to do, but I can't remember what it is. Do you know, Digby, why I am here?'

'No, sir. But I do know you left in a hurry and took your pistols with you.'

By the time he was fully clothed his head was clearer although his legs refused to follow his command. He still felt decidedly shaky, but would come to no harm resting in an armchair to recuperate. Something had spooked him, he would not have brought his pistols otherwise. The sooner he got himself together the better. He sank into an armchair facing the window, from here he had an attractive view of the park, the guest chambers faced southwest and he could watch the sun set over the trees.

A flicker of movement in the trees at the far side of the park attracted his attention. He stiffened, his hands clenched. He remembered, the gang were back and determined to get their revenge on Miss Marsh for removing from their reach the most valuable item they had ever acquired.

He began to push himself out of the chair when he saw something else. He blinked and rubbed his eyes. Surely not! He leaned forward in order to see more clearly; he was not mistaken. Strolling no more than one hundred yards from the intruders was Miss Marsh. She was in grave danger, the men might erupt from the trees and take her captive. What had possessed her to venture out alone? Then she appeared to glance sideways and was racing across the grass as if in fear of her life. She had realised her perilous situation in the nick of time. He watched, his pulse racing, until she disappeared from sight. His breath hissed between his teeth in relief.

'Digby, this place is going to be attacked tonight. I require you to return to The Manor, that too could be a target. I had no idea you would be obliged to join me here, I left a message for you with the butler. Now, I must warn Miss Marsh.' Not allowing the man to protest he pushed himself to his feet and looked around for his walking stick.

* * *

Victoria dashed up the front steps and burst into the vestibule thankful none of the staff were present. The tall clock struck nine o'clock, it would be dark soon; how long would the men hiding in the trees wait before attempting their break-in? She must go and speak to the major, at least he could give her advice even if he was unable to participate himself.

She would gain the sanctuary of her apartment before she was seen by anyone, she had no wish to alarm the rest of the household until absolutely necessary. She was about to step into her private parlour when she was confronted by Major Highcliff, he was fully dressed and, for a man who had appeared to be on his deathbed barely three hours before, looked remarkably robust.

'Miss Marsh, I must speak to you. We can converse out here or we can move in to your sitting-room . . . the choice is yours.'

'You ought not to come into my private apartment, but there is no one here to object, so I suppose there will be no harm in it.'

For a man with only one fully functioning leg he moved fast, before she knew it she was through the door and he had closed it behind him. This was not what she'd expected, he should have left the door wide open and not be leaning against it, staring at her in a most disconcerting way.

Thoroughly discomforted she retreated until the back of her legs made contact with a chair and she fell on to it. What an unpredictable gentleman he was, with no regard for convention at all.

Her pulse slowed and she regained her equilibrium. Why didn't he say something? The fact that she had intended to seek him out in his bedchamber, which would have been breaching the rules of etiquette in a far more serious way, conveniently slipped from her mind.

'What is it you wish to say to me so urgently. I must not entertain you here for longer than necessary.' She stared pointedly at the door closed firmly behind him.

Slowly he approached her. His eyes never left her face, she was pinned to her seat like a butterfly to a board. As he drew closer her fingers gripped the arms and the strange warmth flooded her body. Her throat closed, she couldn't speak. Then he spoke and the spell was broken.

'I came to tell you that the thieves are back, they intend to take their revenge on your household because you deprived them of their most precious asset.' He grabbed a chair and swung it round, then straddled it. 'I take it you saw them and that is why you came back in such a hurry from your ill-advised walk.' She nodded 'Do you not realise, Miss Marsh, that you could have been abducted? What were you thinking of, to venture outside unattended?' He leaned forward to emphasise his point. 'These men are ruthless, it does not bear thinking of what could have happened if they had got their hands on you.'

Enough was enough. He had forgotten a most important fact, she had not been cognisant of their arrival in the vicinity. 'As you can see, sir, I came to no harm. As I had no idea these villains had returned how could I have known they were likely to be in the shrubbery?' She stood up and smiled politely. 'I thank you for your concern but it is unnecessary and unwanted.' Slowly he regained his feet. 'I would not have gone out at all if I had not been so busy in the sickroom taking care of you . . .'

A rush of scalding colour engulfed her from top to toe. What could have possessed her to mention this? Had she not already proved to him she was lacking all sense of decorum. Instead of looking shocked his expression softened, became almost tender.

'My dear, I thought I had dreamed your presence in my bedchamber. Without your intervention I should not be on my feet at all.' He was irresistible when he wasn't cross with her. 'You are a remarkable young woman, I have never met anyone quite like you before.'

He approached her, she knew she should protest, rush into her bedchamber and slam the door in his face, but something held her firm, her feet refused to move. Before she could protest he gathered her close, she could feel his heart thudding against her chest. She leaned back, tilting her head, prepared to demand that he release her but he stopped her words by placing his lips on hers. All desire to struggle vanished as the sweetness of his kiss transported her to a place she had not known existed.

Then she was free, he stepped away and she recovered her composure. Her lips tingled, she was suffused with a delicious warmth. It had not been at all like the unpleasant experience when Mr Lever had attempted to do the same. Of their own volition her thoughts popped out. 'That was most enjoyable, I had not realised being kissed could be so pleasant.'

His mouth dropped. What had she said now to astonish him? He reached out and gently stroked an errant curl from her forehead. 'Sweetheart, I was about to beg your pardon for taking such unwarranted liberties. Instead, might I ask your permission to repeat my transgression?'

'You should not even be in here, sir, and I certainly should not allow you to kiss me for a second time.' Even as she spoke the words she was swaying towards him and his arms encircled her waist, her feet left the boards and his mouth covered hers. This kiss was more demanding, his lips harder; if she had not been in midair her knees would have crumpled beneath her with excitement.

It was he that broke the embrace, setting her down with a sigh. 'My dear, I have ashamedly taken advantage of you but I must not remain here. If Mrs Winterton should come to hear of this no doubt she would have us marching up the aisle before we could draw breath.' He shook his head as if she too would find such an idea not to her liking.

'That would never do, sir, after all we are scarcely suited. You are an older gentleman much set in his ways, no doubt a wife is the last thing you need.' Her voice was strained, this was a highly unsuitable conversation to be having with a gentleman in her private sitting-room in the night.

He stepped away and half smiled, his eyes creased at the corners when he did so. 'I am not so much older than you, I am nine and twenty, but it were not for my dratted leg you might be just the young lady that would suit me, you are intelligent and spirited — one of the prettiest girls I've ever met.'

She was not a brood mare to be considered in this analytical way, he was talking about her as if she was actually offering herself, was dangling for a husband. Her temper rose, it matched her fiery hair.

'I would not marry you if you were the last man available. You are arrogant and dictatorial, in fact you have nothing to recommend you.' Unaccountably her eyes strayed to his damaged leg, she meant nothing by it and quickly looked away. Too late, the damage was done.

His expression changed, his eyes bored into her. She felt her insides shrivel beneath his arctic glare. 'I was not aware that I had made you an offer. I can assure you I would never tie myself to a shrewish girl with no dowry to soften the horror of her sharp tongue.'

His grey glance raked her from top to toe and found her wanting. Then with no further word, he left her parlour taking all hope of a happy outcome to this disaster with him. Angrily she brushed away the tears. He believed her rejection to be because of his infirmity. That was not the reason, she would willingly marry him if he loved her as much she loved him.

Love him? When had this happened? A moment ago she was convinced there was no love on either side.

Disconsolately she sank into the nearest chair; she had made a sad mull of things and now must live with the consequences. How could she repair the rift between them? Would he now return to resume his military career in order to avoid her? The thought of him putting himself in the line of fire brought fresh tears to her eyes, if he should be killed she did not think she could bear the pain it would bring her.

7

Victoria drifted sadly into her bed chamber to remove her garments; it was far too late to ask for a bath to be prepared so she must make do with a strip wash using the jug of water Beth had left out for her. She was now decidedly hungry, all the running about had made her regret she had declined dinner.

Her thoughts were less tangled than they had been before, because something quite extraordinary had belatedly occurred to her. He had kissed her, not once but twice; had quite deliberately closed the door. She was certain such things were not permissible unless those involved were betrothed or already married. He was a gentleman, he would not have taken such liberties if his intentions were not honourable. Also, had he not been larding his conversation with quite unsuitable endearments? Surely this must mean he had feelings for her?

A shiver of excitement rippled through her — however unlikely it might seem, she believed he did intend to pay his addresses. Any other explanation would make him dishonourable, and that she did not believe for a moment. His sharp words were a reflection of his hurt, not his true feelings. From deepest gloom her emotions soared to elation, once they had put this misunderstanding to one side it was possible she would discover he reciprocated her feelings.

She would wait until the kitchen was unoccupied then creep down to make herself a late repast. It was now after nine o'clock; in this household even the housekeeper would have finished her daily tasks and retired to her parlour. Should she dress in something more suitable than her nightgown and wrapper? What if she unexpectedly encountered him when she was in her deshabille? It was more than likely he would, at this very moment, be retrieving his weaponry and double checking the house was quite secure. It would be impossible for anyone to break in with all the shutters fastened.

If he was to be prowling around she had better wait another hour or two before venturing to the kitchen. She would occupy her time by writing up her journal. Never had she had so much excitement in her entire life than she could report for today. When her clock eventually struck eleven she believed it was safe to venture downstairs. The house had been silent for some time, no light shining out on to the terrace below her window.

Her stomach rumbled loudly; if she did not eat soon she would faint clean away. Secure in the knowledge that she would not be seen she tied her bedrobe tightly, checked her hair was hidden under her cap and picked up a candlestick. She did not relish negotiating the dark corridors of the servants' quarters at this late hour so decided to take the main staircase.

Holding her candlestick aloft she stole along the passage that led to the gallery overlooking the main hall. She paused at the top to gather up her skirts, was about to descend, when a noise alerted her. Who could it be at such a time? The faint flicker of a single candle in the passageway that led from the library gave her the answer. The major had been out investigating and was about to limp upstairs and find her, yet again, behaving inappropriately.

She hesitated, her hunger almost overcoming her trepidation. The footsteps were approaching the staircase, she must make a decision. She could not face a second confrontation so retreated as quietly as she'd arrived. His chambers were accessed by the same corridor she must now traverse; her apartment was on the left, his to the right.

She was almost running when she reached the corner. Suddenly a shadowy figure was outlined by her candlelight at exactly the place she must turn. With a squeak of horror she skidded to a halt dropping her candlestick and plunging the area into terrifying darkness. She remained frozen, unable to speak or think coherently. Major Highcliff could not be in two places at once . . . but which one was the intruder?

'Sweetheart, remain where you are, I shall find your candlestick and reignite it for you.'

'Thank God! There's someone coming up the stairs behind me, I thought it was you . . . but . . . '

A strong arm reached out and encircled her shoulders, drawing her close. She could smell the lemon of his shaving soap, feel the smooth touch of his topcoat beneath her fingers.

'Good girl, quietly now, we must go back to my apartment. It is likely they will head for your rooms, you will not be safe there until this matter is dealt with.' His arm tightened. 'Have no fear, I will take care of you.'

This was not the time to protest

about entering a gentleman's rooms, she must rely on his discretion in this further breach of protocol. He seemed able to guide them both without the necessity of a candle. The soft click of the door opening and then she was inside.

'Stay here, my love, I shall deal with the matter. Don't worry, I am quite capable of dealing with these villains even with my infirmity.'

Not waiting for her reply he vanished into the darkness. She definitely heard the sound of him cocking his pistols as he left. She prayed he would be unharmed, that his confidence was not misplaced. After all, a few hours ago he had been most unwell. Also he had been grievously injured and it was many months since he had been in the field of battle.

It was several moments before her eyes adjusted to the dark; the shutters in here were still open and there was sufficient moonlight for her to see her way to a chair. She sank into it, glad her legs had not given out until this very moment.

* * *

How had the devils effected an entry so easily? He had checked every entrance, every window to make sure they were secure. There could be only one explanation, someone had let then in. Toby paused to discard his boots, glad he had lost sufficient weight to make this an easy exercise.

Flattening himself against the wall he listened. Yes! A faint noise approaching told him he was facing two opponents, he had two shots, he must make sure they found their target.

They had inside knowledge, how else would they know the direction of Victoria's apartment? Did this mean that their accomplice was abroad somewhere waiting to offer assistance if need be? Too late to concern himself with such details, he must concentrate on stopping these two before they got any further.

The intruders were almost upon him, the stench of unwashed bodies filled his nostrils. He straightened and stepped into the corridor, silent in stockinged feet. His sudden appearance had the desired effect as the first of the men stopped dead and his companion crashed into him, the candle they were carrying flickered out.

In the confusion it was relatively simple for Toby to knock each one out with the butt of his pistol. All this had been accomplished without a word being exchanged, with luck no one else need know what had taken place.

From the moonlight filtering through the window at the end of the passageway he was able to check that neither of the men were dead. Now he had to secure their hands and have their inert forms transferred to a secure place. Interrogation could not be done at Butterfield, he had no wish to upset the ladies. The only thing he could think that would suffice for rope was his cravat, but this would only restrain one.

The faint flicker of a candle approached. Victoria had come to investigate. His lips curved, she was plucky to the backbone, was prepared to do what most members of the fair sex would shy away from. He still owed her an abject apology for his disgraceful behaviour, her stinging rebuttal of his offer had cut him to the quick. He turned to confirm what he already knew, he was a cripple and of no interest to someone so beautiful she could marry any one she wanted.

* * *

It was too quiet. Surely there should have been sounds of a scuffle, maybe gunshots, but not this eerie silence. Victoria crept forward, although the candle was lit she was holding the brass candlestick firmly in her right hand in order to use it as a weapon if needs be.

Her heart leapt into her throat as a voice whispered to her in the darkness. 'I believe I told you to remain in my chambers. Do you ever do as you are bid, I wonder?'

'I was concerned and came to offer what assistance I might. Good heavens!' In the light from her candle she saw the huddled shapes of two men. 'Have you killed them? Did you use a blade?'

His chuckle filled the darkness. 'What a bloodthirsty young lady you are. No, they are not about to meet their maker . . . at least not at my hands. However, they are unconscious and I need to secure their hands whilst I fetch your grooms to carry them to the stable yard.'

At once she put down the candlestick and removed the belt that tied her bed robe. It had buttons on the bodice so should remain snug about her person. 'Here, we can use this. Shall I tie this one whilst you do the other? Do we not need gags as well? It would be unfortunate if they created a commotion and my aunt were to wake up and find us like this.'

'In which case, my dear girl, we must

remove them before they regain consciousness. Have you ever used a pistol?'

She shook her head, thinking about her earlier decision to stand guard on the house by herself. 'I have not, but I am sure I can point and fire if the occasion should arise.'

'Good girl. You stand guard, they are securely trussed, I don't expect them to wake before I return. In which loft shall I find Tom and Sam?'

'They sleep in the one directly above the tack room, it is accessed by a ladder inside that room.' He turned to go. 'Major, had you better not to put on your boots before venturing outside?'

He muttered something impolite and vanished into the darkness to return with the missing items on. Without further ado he checked both captives were incapable of movement and then, with an airy wave of his hand, he swung away at remarkable speed into the darkness. She strained her ears but was unable to hear him descending the stairs. How was that possible when he used a stick?

It seemed an age before she heard him returning. One of the men had groaned and shown signs of waking up so she'd rammed a strip torn from her nightgown into his mouth. This time the major brought lanterns and two willing accomplices.

'Take one of them between you, I shall remain here until you return.'

'Yes, sir, right away.' Sam seemed to be enjoying the excitement.

He hastily took hold of the shoulders of the man who was now semiconscious and Tom grabbed the feet. They staggered off, the bumping and thumping as they negotiated the staircase echoed back.

'I hope that dreadful racket does not rouse the whole household. I cannot think of a possible explanation that would ever satisfy Aunt Martha.'

'You must return to your own apartment immediately, sweetheart, if anyone comes to investigate I shall be the hero of the hour having overcome two burglars on my own. Only if you are present will there be a difficulty.'

He was correct. 'Goodnight, sir, I believe we shall all be safe after this. No doubt one of these wretches will talk to you in the morning.'

His face was grim as he nodded. 'You can be very sure of it, my love. Interrogation of prisoners is something I am expert in.'

Leaving him to watch the remaining man, who showed no sign of recovery at present, she dashed back to her bed chamber not a moment too soon. She had just closed her parlour door when she heard the housekeeper screeching. It would be only a matter of minutes before the whole house was awake, no one could ignore that cacophony.

She ran into her bed chamber stripping off her bedrobe as she did so. She could not appear in the corridor with her belt missing. Good gracious! What if someone noticed the man was tied with it? Her pulse quickened, then she relaxed, she was almost certain the remaining man was restrained with the major's cravat.

Raised voices and further squeals and screams reverberated throughout the building. Hastily donning her spare robe she ran from the room to try and restore order. Ellie and Mary were clutching each other as if they were about to be murdered at any moment, the housekeeper was sitting on the floor, apparently in a dead faint, and the major had his boot on the back of the intruder in an attempt to stop him wriggling.

Before she had time to intervene he raised his voice to parade ground level and roared. 'Stop that infernal racket this instant.' The girls froze in mid-scream, Bennett jerked from her swoon and the recumbent villain stopped struggling.

'That was well done, sir, if a trifle loud. Pray, allow me to take care of things. Sam and Tom are here and the three of you can remove yourselves forthwith.' Victoria saw his lips thin. Oh dear! He was not a man accustomed to taking orders from anyone. Too late to repine, she could apologise later — it was far more important to restore order in the household before Aunt Martha appeared demanding what was amiss. He had not moved to follow her command. 'Do hurry, sir, did you not hear what I said?'

The major nodded, his jaw rigid. 'I wish to speak to you first thing tomorrow morning, Miss Marsh. Where do you suggest we meet?'

A shiver rippled down her spine, this was one interview she'd much rather avoid. He was quite correct, too frequently she behaved like a shrew when talking to him. Why did he make her behave so out of character? An impulse made her take his hand, his eyes darkened and his fingers closed.

Bennett was now on her feet and the girls recovered from their hysterics and they were gawping at what they saw. He raised her hand and placed it to his lips in a gesture of love. Too late, she was aware they were making a spectacle of themselves.

Her cheeks scarlet she stepped away and covered her confusion by issuing orders. 'Bennett, you may return to your room. See that the girls do so as well. There's no need for you to disturb Mrs Winterton, I shall explain in the morning that there were intruders and that the major apprehended them.' The servants shuffled away without argument.

She all but skipped back to her bed chamber. He had forgiven her as she had him, tomorrow they would put it all behind them and discuss the future. He would ask her to marry him and she would say yes.

8

The two thieves were dumped unceremoniously inside the storeroom and it was secured. Toby banged the door with the end of his cane and winked at Sam. Raising his voice he addressed both grooms as if they were stone deaf. 'They will do for the moment. I shall need daylight to interrogate them. I shall also need a red-hot branding iron and a pair of pincers.'

The two men grinned and joined in gleefully. 'I'll get a good fire burning first thing, not something we can do in the dark.'

Tom nodded to his friend. 'Better to do it at dawn, sir, you'll not want to distress the ladies with their screaming.'

Certain his captives would have overheard their conversation, Toby replied, 'Away to your beds, thank you for a good night's work. I shall see you both here at five o'clock in the morning.' He moved so that they were out of earshot. 'Sam, you ride first thing to The Manor and tell Mr Digby what has transpired here.'

He retraced his steps, his mind busy. He would discover where the other members of this nefarious gang were holed-up and then John could deal with it when he returned. Miss Marsh ... no, he would think of her as Victoria in future ... would understand if he was obliged to postpone their meeting.

If anyone had thought to ask him his views on marriage two weeks ago he would have said he desired it is much as a sword through his shoulder, that he had insufficient income to support a wife and little chance of resuming his command.

Amazingly everything was changed; he could resume his career and had met the girl he wished to marry. He was not sure he was ready for it. He would probably make a poor husband, she was right to call him dictatorial, he'd spent his adult life in the military and expected to be obeyed instantly. He knew nothing of the softer side of things, had no notion how to please a lady and little wherewithal to keep her in the kind of luxury she would no doubt expect.

He felt happier than he had in months, no, if he was honest happier than he had ever felt. Whatever the obstacles they would overcome them, somehow he would persuade her that they were the perfect match. He shrugged. No point in worrying, problems had a way of solving themselves after a good night's sleep.

He hobbled back to his chamber, his leg protesting at the punishment he'd given it these past few hours. Once in his bed he closed his eyes and was on the brink of oblivion when he jackknifed. Good grief! There was still one of the gang at large, the person who had unlocked the door. How could he have forgotten this? Was Victoria still in danger? Would, whoever it was, make a further attempt on her person whilst she slept or go outside to release the prisoners?

* * *

Victoria could not settle. After all the excitement she was wide awake and still had not been down to the kitchen to find something to eat. Scrambling out of bed for the third time, she headed for her closet. The tinderbox was kept on the shelf and she could find it with her eyes closed. Moments later she had sufficient illumination to strip off her night apparel and get dressed.

This time she would go down fully clothed, she'd breached enough rules of etiquette tonight and have no wish to cause further comment, have his eyebrows shoot up under his hair in that endearing way he had, in the unlikely event that he was in the kitchen on the same errand as herself.

Taking the main staircase she walked

without fear to the rear of the house. Good, the range was still alight, if she stirred it vigorously and added more coal she could boil a kettle and make herself some tea. This task completed she headed for the pantry where the fresh food was kept on cool, slate shelves.

She cut herself three slices of bread, added some butter and cheese and a large dollop of tomato relish. Was this sufficient? No, she would have a generous wedge of plum cake as well. She placed the feast she'd assembled on a suitable tray and carried it through to the kitchen.

The kettle was hissing gently on the trivet and she put her food on the table whilst she assembled the makings for her tea. Eventually she sat to begin her midnight supper. The bread was poised in front of her mouth when she quite clearly heard heavy footsteps approaching. There was no doubt as to who it was, this time the sound of his cane rapping on the floorboards was evident.

With a sigh she put the food down and braced herself. The door swung open and the major burst in. 'Thank God! I thought they had taken you.'

Had he run mad? She could not restrain her giggle. 'Why ever should you think I had been abducted? And, more to the point, how did you know my bed chamber was unoccupied?'

His cheeks reddened under her scrutiny. He shifted uncomfortably and ran his finger around his neck cloth. It was only then she noticed he was dressed somewhat haphazardly, no waistcoat under his topcoat and his cravat knotted any old how. Something had made him leap from his bed to dress in such a hurry.

Not waiting for him to answer she jumped up and pointed to a chair on the opposite side of the table to her own. 'Please sit down, you must be exhausted. No, do not explain it to me now. I shall get you a cup of tea and something to eat. After we have eaten you can tell me what it was that alarmed you.'

His smile made her insides somersault. 'I have not eaten since this morning. Until you mentioned it I had not realised how hungry I am.'

She hurried back to the pantry and assembled him a similar repast, but added extra bread and cheese and several slices of ham. His eyes widened when she placed the laden tray in front of him, but he made no comment. She handed him a cup of tea and sat down. 'I must eat, please forgive me but I tend to be . . .'

'Argumentative? Wilful? Impulsive?' His expression was affectionate, his eyes danced with amusement. He was irresistible when he wished to be so.

'I was going to say, before you so rudely interrupted me, that I can be a little short tempered.'

His bark of laughter caused her to slop her tea into the saucer. 'Botheration! You are a most unpredictable gentleman, I cannot make you out at all. Now, kindly behave yourself and let me eat my supper.'

When she was done she pushed away the plate with a sigh of satisfaction. Reaching out to pick up her teacup she glanced upwards to see that he had finished his meal and was watching her, a slight smile playing around his lips.

'I beg your pardon, sir, I'm afraid you have seen me at my worst. When I am hungry I can't make idle conversation, but I am now ready to listen.'

He raised his cup as if in a salute. 'I am certain that someone in your household is in league with those villains. How else could they know the whereabouts of your bedchamber or how to effect an entry into a securely locked house?'

Her stomach lurched and she wished she had not eaten so much. 'Why have we been sitting here this past half hour when the villain could be about to attack us?'

'My love, do not distress yourself. As you only have female staff inside, it must be one of them so we are in no real danger at this present time.'

'How can that be? I believe all the staff here to be loyal to my aunt and myself. They are well paid and certainly not overworked, why should they wish to risk everything in this way?'

'I doubt it is any of the established members, there must be someone who has joined your household recently?'

She considered. 'Yes, there is one who came to us only a few weeks ago, the scullery maid, May. But she is a little dab of a thing, I can hardly credit she is part of a bloodthirsty gang of thieves.'

'Would she know the whereabouts of your rooms?'

'I don't see any reason why she shouldn't, it's hardly a secret. Any one of the chambermaids would tell her what she wished to know. She shares an attic bedroom with the kitchen maid, her absence would be noticed.'

'I have found no evidence of a forced entry, therefore it will have been she who left a door unlocked.'

He pushed his chair back and smiled

down at her, resting one hand on her shoulder. She shivered beneath his touch, found herself compelled to rise. His arms enfolded her and this time she went willingly, gazing up at him, her heart pounding. His eyes burned into her and he lowered his head to cover her mouth with his own. Waves of pleasure spiralled down her spine and her hands crept around his neck of their own volition.

'No, my love, this will not do.' Gently he removed her fingers but retained them inside his own. 'I find you quite irresistible, but I should not — must not — let my feelings lead me to take liberties.'

'I wished you to kiss me, if anyone was at fault it was me. I find that you have a most peculiar effect on me, I do not understand it at all, I'm not sure that I even like you very much.'

'Do not fight it, sweetheart, something extraordinary has happened to both of us. I truly believe angel dust was sprinkled on us whilst we were in the church that fateful morning.' He raised her hands and kissed each palm in turn, then she was free. 'That was an excellent supper. At least we have one thing we share, my dear, we both enjoy our food.'

His light-hearted remark brought home to her as nothing else could have that she had fallen in love with a man she barely knew. This was not how she had thought things would be. Where was the romance, the love, the flowers and the courtship that should go hand-in-hand with such a momentous occasion?

She tried to step around him but somehow he managed to be blocking her path. Her throat was clogged, her cheeks were wet and she could offer no explanation. To her astonishment he gently brushed her tears away.

'I am sorry if I have upset you, little one, we must talk tomorrow when we are both rested, neither of us will make sensible decisions tonight.'

Toby could not bear to see her so

discomfited. 'And as soon as I am signed off by the quack I shall be returning to Spain to rejoin my regiment. I shall no longer be here to plague you with my unwanted attentions.'

Her cheeks paled at his words. 'Please, I do not wish you to return before you are fully recovered. I have no wish for you to put yourself in danger in order to spare my sensibilities.' She stared earnestly at him and his heart almost leapt from his chest. 'Indeed, if I'm honest I do not wish you to return to the front line at all.'

He had not been mistaken, she did have feelings for him. The lowness of spirits that had followed him like a black dog these past months finally dropped from his shoulders. A new life opened up in front of him — a life full of happiness to be shared with this lovely girl. He didn't want her to go — for the first time in his life he wanted to make small talk. 'You have not finished your tea, do not hurry off, please remain here and converse with me a little while longer.'

Without hesitation she walked back and resumed her seat. His lips twitched as he noticed that, although she was correctly attired, her hair hung in a single braid down her back. He had an almost irresistible urge to release it and run his fingers through its lustrous length, kissing her was not enough. Pushing such nonsense the back of his mind he sat down and tried to think of something mundane to discuss.

She waited, her beautiful green-brown eyes fixed on him, quite unaware of the impact she was making. Then she jerked forward sending the cups flying. 'I had quite forgotten, the burglars will know that Sir John is away from home. I sent a warning, but I do not know if it was heeded.'

'I have the matter in hand, sweetheart. I sent Digby back to ensure the butler and footmen are fully armed and remain on watch tonight.' He took her hands, they were all but lost in his. The skin was soft under his calloused, battle hardened fingers. This would not do, time enough tomorrow for such things. 'You must not worry, my love, allow me to protect you, it is what I do best.'

She nodded and smiled tremulously, then gently withdrew her fingers. 'I must return to my apartment, it is highly regular to be sitting here like this.'

'There's one thing more I must ask you to do before you retire. Kindly go upstairs to the attic and bring that girl down to me.'

She stared at him as if he was an escapee from Bedlam. 'I cannot possibly do that. Imagine the noise she will make, she will rouse the household again and this time we will have no other recourse but to explain the whole. My aunt might well have a relapse if she discovers the house was invaded in this way. I have no wish to tell her until she has breakfasted.'

'I'm afraid it must be done.'

Victoria smiled and something most

peculiar happened. He was little more than a cripple, whatever his personal feelings he must never reveal that his thoughts had turned to marriage. Like a bolt from the blue he had fallen head over ears in love with her. It had not been merely desire that had made him kiss her. He was glad about that.

Grinning like a schoolboy he stood up. Now she must truly think him deranged. He schooled his features, but could not stop his eyes from expressing his emotion. He thanked God that she seemed more preoccupied in the task he had given her than in how he was behaving.

'I shall go up at once, where shall I bring her? Do you wish to speak to her in here?'

'In the library, the more formal the interview the better. Here she would be more comfortable, I wish her to be so terrified she reveals everything.'

9

It was fortuitous, Victoria thought, that she had got dressed before venturing to the kitchen. She could hardly snatch May from her bed if she was still in her night robe. It took her some time to locate the room as she rarely had cause to venture into the attics. Should she knock or march straight in? She decided on the latter, after all she had the right to enter where she pleased without notice.

She had a lantern as it gave more light and was easier to manage in the narrow passageways than a candlestick. She lifted the latch and stepped in, holding it up. The kitchen maid sat bolt upright, clutching the covers under her chin.

'Lawks, miss, you fair gave me a turn. Is the house on fire?'

May remained hidden beneath the

covers, obviously a sounder sleeper then her roommate. 'No, Josey, Major Highcliff wishes to speak to May most urgently. There was an attempted burglary earlier, and he believes May left the door open for them. There's nothing for you to worry about.' They both stared at the unmoving hump.

'I'll give her a poke, Miss Marsh. She ain't usually so slow to wake.'

Victoria was unsurprised when the blankets were pulled back to reveal a bolster lying where May should have been. She was too late, the girl had flown, but had she left before the men came in or was she at very moment releasing them? 'The girl must have run away knowing she would be apprehended for her part in tonight's events. Go back to sleep, I shall tell the major that May is not here.'

It was imperative that she warn him, he must go outside and make sure the prisoners were still secure. The back stairs emerged adjacent to the boot-room door, she realised it would be far quicker for her to run to the stable yard than for the major to limp out there himself.

Decision made, she dashed to the door and found it unbolted. Even if she met May she was half a head taller and considerably stronger, it would be simple enough to overpower her. Only as she reached the archway that led into the cobbled yard did it occur to her that it might not be just the girl she had to face. The two men could well have been set free by now and be waiting for her.

* * *

Toby reached for his pocket watch. He cursed under his breath when he recalled he had left it attached to his waistcoat, which he was not wearing. He could get up and go and look at the tall clock in the hallway, but was too tired and it was a long way from the library to the servant sleeping quarters. He had probably set his recovery back by several weeks with all the unaccustomed activity.

He smiled, the longer he spent in the neighbourhood the better, it would give him the opportunity to pay court to Victoria.

It must be a full quarter of an hour since she'd gone to fetch the miserable servant girl; what was keeping her? With a sigh he decided he'd better go and investigate. The thought of navigating the narrow staircase that led up to the attic filled him with foreboding.

Gritting his teeth, he pushed himself upright and tentatively leaned his weight on his injured right leg. He winced, it hurt like the very devil. Still, there was always a silver lining to every problem. If he hadn't been lame he would never have knocked the books to the floor in the church and Victoria wouldn't have come over to help him.

Ignoring the pain he swung steadily through the house and into the narrower passageways that led to the stairs he required. He passed a doorway and a draft of cool night air made his skin prickle with apprehension. There was an open door; it could only mean one thing. But had someone come in or was this the way the girl had escaped?

There was a light clatter of footsteps behind him, he was expecting to see Victoria but it was one of the serving girls, more or less correctly dressed. 'Has Miss Marsh been upstairs with you?'

'Yes, sir, but she's gone to find you. That May has run off.'

He had missed Victoria, she must have taken a different route to him. May had left by the open door. Far more important was the fact that the scullery maid could already be releasing the men.

'What is your name?'

'Josey, sir. I came down to see if I could be of any assistance.'

'Indeed you can, you must lock the door behind me, but remain vigilant. I shall return this way, but do not open it to anyone else. Is that quite clear?' The girl nodded obviously enjoying the unaccustomed excitement. He handed her his lantern; he had no need of it for it was already less dark than it had been an hour ago. Perfectly good visibility for someone with his excellent night vision.

Outside he forgot his infirmity, once again he was an officer in command. He set out steadily, taking the longer route round; he would be more likely to surprise his quarry if he arrived from the direction of the house and not via the back route.

* * *

Victoria hid her lantern beneath the folds of her skirt, better not to alert anyone of her coming. It did not occur to her to turn back, she was the only one who could prevent the villains from escaping.

Using the shadows to good advantage she slipped into the stable yard and pressed herself against the bricks. The place appeared deserted, no unusual noises, just the expected rustling and munching of the horses in the loose boxes.

She held her breath and listened more carefully.

Yes, she detected a faint sound coming from the store next to the tack room. On tiptoes she crossed the yard, glad she was wearing her indoor slippers, they would be quite ruined by this experience but she could be certain her approach was silent.

She put her ear against the door. The hair on the back of her neck stood to attention. Harsh whispers, and what could only be the sound of someone untying ropes, were clear. Without hesitation she rammed the bolts back and stepped away.

Her heart was pounding, her hands clammy — what should she do now? Should she call for aid? If she did so it would tell the villains they had been imprisoned by a female. Would this give them the courage to smash down the door?

There was someone behind her. Before she could move, two arms like bands of steel came around her chest and lifted her from the ground. Her bladder all but emptied from the shock.

She breathed in and instantly relaxed. An inappropriate bubble of mirth escaped and his arms relaxed and she was dropped with a decided thump to the cobbles.

The hands transferred to her shoulders and spun her round. 'Good grief, my love, what in the name of heaven are you doing out here? I could have injured you, I thought you the missing girl.'

'May escaped and came out to release her friends. I have locked all three of them into the storeroom. Did I not do well?'

She felt tremors ripple through him and knew he was laughing. 'I should shake some sense into you, young lady. You put yourself in grave danger, those men could have attacked you if you had arrived a few moments later.

'But they didn't, so there's no point in debating the issue.'

The pressure on her shoulders increased, he was not restraining her but using her to keep his balance. 'Please allow me to help you. Only a few hours ago you were seriously ill with a bout of fever.'

'How perspicacious of you, my dear. However, I can manage to get myself back inside, I would not dream of using you to aid me. You have done more than enough tonight.'

'Stuff and nonsense! If you're wondering what others might think, it's far too late for that. We have thoroughly disregarded all conventions these past few hours after all, why should we behave sensibly at this late stage?'

'In which case, my dear, I should be grateful for your able assistance.'

She led him towards the side door, becoming more concerned with each step they took as the weight on her shoulders became heavier. If he swooned she would be unable to support him, he was a formidable height and he must be double her own weight.

Somehow they reached the door and he rapped on it and demanded entry. Who could possibly be waiting to let them in? The bolts were run back and Josey, bless her, was there to greet them. Between them they got him as far as the drawing-room.

'You must rest here, Major Highcliff, Josey has gone to fetch you a pillow and a blanket. I'm sure you have slept in worse places whilst on campaign on the Peninsula.'

Just as the girl returned with the bedding he chose to reply. 'I have, my dearest love, but never with so fair a companion at my side.'

Victoria carefully pushed the pillow under his head and dragged a blanket over his long form, his breathing steadied and she knew he was asleep.

Josey spoke from beside her. 'Fancy that! Did you hear what he called you, Miss Marsh?'

Victoria was still glowing from the endearment, the more time she spent with this wonderful man the more she loved him. And she was almost certain he returned the sentiment, otherwise why would he lard his conversation with such words? 'Major Highcliff and I are betrothed.'

What had possessed her to say such a thing when it had not yet been discussed between them? It had been her heart speaking her thoughts out loud. The words were out, it was too late to retract them. She would have to warn the major when she spoke to him tomorrow.

'Engaged to the major? Fancy that! I never knew the like! To fall in love in such a short space of time — who would have thought it possible and he a military gentleman as well?'

'Major Highcliff has not yet spoken to Mrs Winterton, so can I have your word that you will not mention this to anyone until he has?'

The girl curtsied and nodded before returning to her attic room leaving Victoria to check everything. It would have been so much easier if Digby had not been sent to protect Toby's nieces and nephews. She almost tripped over her feet in shock. When had he become Toby and not the more formal Major Highcliff?

As she climbed the central staircase she mulled over what had happened. Who would have thought it? That was indeed what everyone would say after he had declared his love and made her an offer. There was a small moment of doubt when she settled down for the night. He was a soldier, surely they were not prone to such flights of fancy as falling in love in a matter of days? If he was intending to speak to her about matrimony tomorrow why had he not given her a hint this evening? Could she have mistaken the matter, was he merely flirting with her?

★   ★   ★

The rattle of her morning chocolate woke her from a deep slumber. She yawned and stretched and rolled over to look at the mantel clock. It was after nine — she was disgracefully tardy. Beth could be heard tipping water in the dressing-room. Excellent, she could not possibly get dressed until she had completed her ablutions.

Ignoring her drink she hurried through to the maid. 'If the water is cool enough for me to step into, I shall take my bath immediately. There's no need to have any more water fetched.'

The girl bobbed. 'What shall I lay out for you this morning, miss?'

'The pale green dimity with the emerald green sash and matching slippers. And I shall need assistance with my hair this morning, if you have the time.'

In less than half an hour Victoria was ready, she examined her appearance from all sides in the full length glass and was satisfied. It would not do to look anything but perfect when receiving her first formal offer of marriage however peculiar the circumstances. At some time during the night she had decided she had no reason to doubt him, his intentions were of the most honourable.

Bennett waylaid her in the vestibule. 'Miss Marsh, you've missed a deal of excitement. Sir John arrived and he and the major put those varmints in a diligence and took them away. The major and Madam were closeted together for an age.'

Victoria's spirits dropped. Toby had left without speaking to her, did this mean he had changed his mind or that he put duty before his personal feelings? 'Thank you, I shall take breakfast later. We shall have to see about appointing a new scullery maid, as the girl was in league with the robbers.'

'Such a shame, I can't bear to think that someone as young as her could be so wicked. Will she be transported?'

'We must leave it to the magistrate to decide her fate, but I shall pray that she is treated mercifully.'

She had no option but to go and speak to Aunt Martha who always sat in the small drawing-room as it received the morning sun, she was not looking forward to this interview one jot. She must pretend it was love on both sides when she was only certain of her own feelings. She could never let her aunt know they had been intimate before any mention of marriage.

'There you are, Victoria. I have been waiting all morning to congratulate you. Such a handsome man, and so well-connected. I never thought you to be the impulsive sort, but here you are betrothed to a man you barely know.'

Victoria had difficulty keeping the shock from her face. How could she be betrothed when he had not spoken to her? She could not reveal her disquiet, she must go along with it, pretend she was fully cognisant of the fact that she was to marry the man who had not made her an offer.

'We knew the moment our eyes met across the church. Our feelings are so strong, and there is no need for delay on either side.'

'How romantic — he is a true gentleman and exactly the sort of man I hoped one day you would meet and fall in love with. It's a great shame about his leg, but no doubt it will improve with time.'

10

Toby decided to concentrate on discovering the whereabouts of the rest of the thieves. Discussion of his future matrimonial plans could wait until this matter was resolved. It had been a most enlightening hour he'd spent with Mrs Winterton. With hindsight he supposed he should have spoken to Victoria before telling her aunt that they were to be married. His mouth curved, she would understand, she was not the sort of girl to worry about such niceties. Hadn't he made his feelings clear in the way he had behaved last night?

He had no wish to be bandying words with his brother-in-law or sister on the subject of his marriage when there was this matter of grave importance to deal with. The diligence had just rattled to a halt at the rear of the stables as he and John cantered up.

'I wish to interrogate the girl first, John. Is there somewhere out here I can use?'

'Don't be too harsh with her, she's scarcely more than a child.'

'I'm not a brute, I shall handle her gently, but I think I will gain information from her that will make things far easier with the other two. Now, where shall I do this?'

He was directed to a small office used by the estate manager when dealing with tenant farmers and their problems. It was ideal, having two solid chairs and a table and nothing else. He positioned himself behind the table and waited for two sturdy gardeners to bring in the girl. John hurried off to organise his men in the search that would come later, once he had the information he needed.

May was more carried than marched and crouched back on the chair staring at him with huge eyes, her ashen cheeks tear streaked. He hated to subject the poor little thing to more distress, and he wished it could be possible to release her once he had the information he required.

'Well, girl, you do realise you could be sent to the gallows for your part in the attempted burglary?'

She gulped and nodded but was unable to offer a coherent answer. Keeping his expression severe he continued. 'However if you are prepared to tell me how you came to be involved with those two villains it is possible some leniency might be shown to you.'

This remark stirred her into speech. 'Bill's my sweetheart, I ain't telling you nothing else so don't ask.'

Toby realised he was dealing with someone far tougher than he'd supposed, this was no vulnerable girl, but a hardened criminal like the rest of the gang. Her distress was because she'd been caught, not because she was overcome with remorse.

She sniffed and wiped her dripping nose on her apron and stared at him belligerently. 'I ain't sorry I let them in, I've done it before, I likes to get the better of you toffs. You treat us like dirt, as if we're worth nothing.'

He had no wish to employ his more drastic interrogation methods on this girl, she might be part of the gang but she was still little more than a child. He banged his cane on the floor and the scullery maid was removed and her paramour was dragged in.

'Your intended will dance at the end of a rope along with you and your friend unless you tell me the whereabouts of your comrades.'

This statement caused the noxious creature to stiffen but his red rimmed eyes glared back quite unrepentant. 'You ain't tricking me that way, mister, do yer worst. I'm staying mum.'

For all his bravado Toby detected a hesitation in the man's statement. He slammed his hands down and shot forward so that his face was inches from his captive. The stench almost made him gag. 'Very well. Have it your way.

The girl can go to the gallows. Sir John is the magistrate, I have his authority to dispatch her directly to jail.'

He dropped back into his chair and picked up a quill, dipped it in a leisurely fashion in the inkwell and began writing as if he were indeed signing the poor girl's death warrant. He prayed his pretence would be effective. The sooner this matter could be settled the better. The clatter of several horses outside in the yard meant John was ready to leave, and as soon as he had the whereabouts of the rest of the gang his part in this would be over.

'All right, mister, Just give me your word my girl will not die,' he said.

Toby kept his face lowered until he could school his features, appear unmoved by this statement. It was strange, before his unexpected encounter with Victoria he would not have believed it possible that love could work where violence did not. 'I'm waiting now. Tell me where will we find the others?'

The demoralised wretch slumped further into his chair dropping his face on to his chest in despair. 'It ain't her fault, sir, she were helping me.'

Soon Toby had all the information needed for the capture of the gang that had been terrorising the neighbourhood for the past few weeks. 'Well, that was a job well done, John, don't you think? I've not had so much excitement since I left the regiment last year.'

His brother-in-law slapped him heartily on the shoulder. 'I should hope not, old fellow. Celia and I are delighted to find you back to your old self at last. We don't want to hear any more of that tomfoolery about resigning your commission, you are surely more than ready to resume command of your troops.'

'I believe that I am, in mind certainly, but my leg still needs longer to recover. I have no intention of returning for a few months yet.' Was now the opportune moment to tell John that he was all but engaged to Victoria?

Victoria could not postpone her visit to the kitchen any longer. It was her duty to speak to Cook and reassure her that she would not be dismissed because of the actions of the girl she had chosen to employ. It was still hard to credit that May had been involved in something nefarious. In a few weeks she had been with them she had shown no sign of her proclivities, although Cook had said the girl was sometimes a mite surly.

Victoria had done her best to improve matters since her arrival three years ago, indeed, the house was much cleaner, the food better and the laundry done on time. However the indoor staff had been with Aunt Martha this age and were not going to change their ways because of anything she might say to them. So the household continued to drift along and would need someone with more steel in their backbone to shake them out of their lethargy. Her eyes glinted, if Major Highcliff was in permanent residence they would have no option but to improve.

They were not expected at The Manor until five o'clock, it was now a little after noon. How could she fill the hours until she went to her chamber to change? Perhaps she would walk into the village and spend time with Marybeth. No, if she did that she would be obliged to discuss her betrothal and she was not ready to do that, even with her closest friend.

Her aunt was going through the menus with the housekeeper, after that her elderly relative would retire to her bed chamber for her afternoon rest. What could she do? She had no inclination to write in her journal, or to finish the watercolour she had begun last week. Restlessly she prowled the house until inspiration struck. She would put on her new riding habit and take her docile mare out for an amble in the sunshine.

She had been gone no more than half an hour when she saw a horse and she spied the major racing towards her. She reined back, the major had obviously had the same idea as her.

She watched his mount take two hedges in its stride; the major was a remarkable horseman considering he was infirm.

Her mare showed unaccustomed spirit, dancing and whinnying as the gelding thundered across the meadow. He brought his horse to rearing halt beside her.

'My dear, I saw you riding this way and decided to join you. I hope you have no objection?'

His cheeks were flushed from the exertion and his eyes held an expression she did not recognise.

'I am truly delighted to see you, sir, but should you be gallivanting all over the countryside? Would you not be better resting . . . allowing your leg to fully recover?'

He ignored her comment. 'Come, sweetheart, let us ride into the wood over there, it will be far cooler in the shade.' Allowing her no time to voice an opinion he positioned his mount so that her mare was obliged to follow.

They stopped in a small clearing and he turned to her, his expression earnest. 'Actually, I was on my way to Butterfield Hall. There's something I most particularly wish to say to you before this evening.'

Victoria was as unsettled as her horse. 'Have you spoken to Sir John and Lady Farnham about what took place last night?'

'No, my sister was too busy with her mother-in-law who has arrived for an unexpected visit, and Sir John rode out with his men to capture the remaining members of the gang. Shall we return to your home together?'

She nodded. It could only be one thing he wished to say to her in private, she was dizzy with excitement. Barely a word was exchanged between them on the short ride, whatever it was he wished to say to her he obviously had no intention of saying it out here.

Sam was waiting outside in the gravelled turning circle and she kicked her foot free and dropped lightly to the ground, not bothering to wait for her companion. He could go and speak to Aunt Martha whilst she went upstairs and changed into something more suitable.

Toby completed his dismount without mishap and tossed the reins to a waiting stable boy. 'I shall be here a while, untack him and see that he's comfortable.' Why had his beloved rushed off without him? He frowned. His leaving without seeing her this morning had been maladroit, he must smooth things over, but how could he mend his fences without revealing how he felt and putting her in an impossible position?

Knowing that he loved her might frighten her away. He was going to get it right, if he couldn't go down on one knee he intended to make her a formal offer, show her he was serious in his intention to marry her. However, he must make it clear he would not coerce her in, that she was free to proceed or withdraw at any time.

His mouth quirked. That was not strictly correct, he had never been gainsaid in his life nor had he lost a battle and this was one he was determined to win however long it took to achieve his aim.

11

Victoria rang the bell vigorously to summon her maid. She would change into her smartest ensemble, it had but recently arrived from the modiste and she had yet to wear it. 'Quickly, I must complete my ablutions and return downstairs immediately. Put out my new yellow silk if you please.'

Her hair had to be redressed and this took an unconscionable time, she had been upstairs far too long and she had yet to put on her gown. Her abigail settled the confection to her satisfaction and stepped back to admire the result.

'You look a picture, Miss Marsh. Shall you put on the bonnet and take the parasol?'

Victoria stared wistfully at the matching narrow brimmed bonnet with the fetching bunch of cherries. Should she take her parasol? It had caused quite a stir when she'd strolled down the village street. She frowned as she twirled it between her fingers. She tapped her foot, admiring her half kid boots which were dyed exactly the same shade of buttercup yellow.

'I will put on my bonnet and take the parasol after all, also I shall need my gloves. I shall suggest to the major that we take a walk in the garden, not remain inside.' Confident that she looked her best she left her bed chamber. The clock in the hall struck one, good gracious she'd kept her betrothed kicking his heels down stairs for over an hour and he was not a patient man.

*   *   *

Toby was returning to the drawing-room after an entertaining hour talking to his future great aunt when he heard a door bang somewhere at the back of the house and then light footsteps. At last, his beloved girl was coming down to speak to him. He waited in the shadows wishing to be able to observe without being seen himself.

To his astonishment she was wearing a bonnet, her gloves, and carrying a parasol. She never failed to astound him, life with her would never be predictable. A surge of love filled him, all he could think was how lucky he was to have met her. Maybe if he'd asked the Almighty to intervene in his life earlier he might have been acquainted with this wonderful girl some weeks ago. One thing was certain, however bleak things might be in the future, he'd never doubt the existence of a supreme power. He'd been given a chance of happiness, he was not going to let that slip away.

'Victoria, you are like a ray of sunshine floating down the stairs.'

Her eyes met his and the intensity of her smile almost unmanned him. There was something most particular he had to say to her, and nothing was going to stop him. He held out his hand and she floated down the stairs to place her own in his. He tucked it through his arm and prepared to lead her into the drawing-room.

'I thought we could go and sit in the arbour in the rose garden, sir, it's far too clement today to remain inside.' He smiled down at her, his expression teasing. 'Perhaps that would be better, I believe your parasol and bonnet would be redundant in the drawing-room.' He nodded sagely. 'Might I be allowed to say that both items are quite stunning, and brand new perhaps?'

She peeped from under the brim, her eyes alight with laughter. 'You have found me out. I could not bear to wear the dress without the matching accessories. Therefore we must converse while taking a stroll in the garden or I shall look ridiculous.'

His hand tightened over hers and his eyes darkened. 'You look ravishing, my love, and I appreciate the effort you have made for me.'

It was her turn to tease him. 'La, sir, do you know nothing about young ladies? We dress to impress ourselves, and a gentleman's opinion is always secondary to our own.'

'You are a baggage, my love, and it's time someone took you in hand.'

Toby guided her to the front door and out into the sunshine but he hesitated on the top step. He had been obliged to lean heavily on her in order to walk steadily, for some reason he was without his walking stick.

'Major, what have you done with your cane?'

'Unfortunately in my dash across country to join you it must have become dislodged from its position behind the saddle. I shall have to obtain a replacement.' He smiled down at her in that particular way of his and she forgave him his impolite remark. 'Now, you must guide me to the bower, I hope it is not over far, for both our sakes.'

She stopped and stared earnestly up at him. 'This is ridiculous. I will not drag you across the garden in order to satisfy my vanity. Let us repair to the drawing-room. I shall remove my bonnet and discard my parasol.'

His fingers tightened on her arm and she felt a thrill of excitement ripple through her. 'Thank you, sweetheart, I promise that in a week or two I shall no longer be such a weakling. It has been a particularly exhausting twenty four hours, and I am ashamed to admit that until recently I took little exercise, but moped around the house feeling sorry for myself.'

Her eyes brimmed, there could not be another gentleman in the whole world who would admit he was less than in perfect health. 'I care not about your leg; you are the bravest man I know and I applaud you for it.'

He escorted her into the drawing-room and this time he closed the door firmly behind him. She sank gracefully on to the sofa and sat with lowered eyes, waiting expectantly for her first offer.

He cleared his throat and shifted uncomfortably. 'I apologise that I cannot do this in the traditional manner.'

He bowed deeply and then leaned down to collect her hands in his. 'My angel, will you do me the inestimable honour of becoming my wife? Unlikely as it may seem, I have fallen head over ears in love with you and wish to marry you at the earliest possible moment.'

She didn't hesitate. 'I accept your kind offer. Ridiculous as it may seem to others, I believe that I knew the moment I saw you across the church last week that you were the man I have been waiting for.'

Gently he pulled her to her feet and cupped her face, tilting it gently towards him. She stretched upon tiptoes and threaded her fingers through his thick hair. This time his kiss was different, something deeper, more loving passed between them. He raised his head and his eyes burned into hers. Finally she understood why men and women did such foolish things in the name of love.

'My darling, I must take my leave, I have to tell my family the good news. I shall count the minutes until you join me this evening for dinner.' He pulled off her gloves impatiently and then kissed each of her fingers in turn. A touch of his lips on her burning skin made her knees tremble.

'I wish you to call me by my given name, my love, we are both so beyond the pale I can't believe so small a breach of etiquette will bother our family one jot.'

'Toby it shall be; and as you have been calling me anything but Miss Marsh, using my given name will be an improvement.'

'I feel like a young man again, no longer someone past his prime. I have watched others in my regiment succumb but never thought I would be struck down.' He grinned lopsidedly. 'If I am honest, my darling, I did not believe there was any such thing as love until we met.'

'I know what you mean. I have had a dozen or more suitors paraded before me this past year and could not understand why I felt nothing at all for them. I believe that our meeting was preordained, we are truly meant to be together.'

In response he drew her close again and dropped a feather light kiss on her parted lips. 'I must go. John and Celia will think I have run mad racing off as I did without a word. Dinner tonight can be a celebration of our betrothal as well as our successful mission.' His expression changed to one of sadness. 'I have no ring to give you, but I promise you I shall find you something as beautiful as you are next time I am in town.'

'I have no need of such baubles, but there's something you must understand, my love. We cannot be married until I have found someone to be companion to my aunt. She took me in when I was destitute. She is the only family that I have. I fear it will take many months to discover a person she will accept. Of course, there is a simple solution to this problem.'

His eyes blazed. 'I am your family now, sweetheart. However, I do understand your reluctance to leave. I am certain things will come about to our satisfaction, suitable arrangements will eventually be made.'

* * *

Against all her expectations he loved her, she was to have a happy union after all. It was hard not being able to tell her aunt that she had only just received his offer when Aunt Martha believed them to have been engaged the night before.

'Aunt Martha, I could not be happier, my only concern now is how we shall live, for I know that he is not a wealthy man. Would you have any objection if we made our home with you?'

Her aunt laughed merrily. 'You have no need to worry about your finances, my dear girl. You are my sole heir, you will be a very wealthy young woman when I am gone.' Shocked Victoria sank on to a nearby chair, she had never considered herself an heiress. 'I had a long conversation with your young man whilst you were still abed. I have agreed to settle ten thousand pounds on you when you marry. That should be more than sufficient to keep you in style until you eventually inherit the remainder of my estate.'

Almost overnight Toby had been transformed from a man of no substance to a gentleman of fortune. That was why he had come up to scratch, his talking of loving her was a mere ploy. Bitter disappointment engulfed her, she must not show her feelings and spoil the moment for her aunt. His behaviour had extinguished her happiness; like an autumn bonfire which turned the beauty of the leaves to ashes; so too were all her dreams dashed and destroyed.

She must not let her aunt know her misery. Victoria went over and hugged the frail, old lady. 'You are too generous, but there's no need to worry about the money. It is to be a long engagement, and anyway I have no intention of leaving you alone until I have found you a companion.'

Victoria was well aware that her great

aunt disliked having strangers under her roof, no doubt it would take a wonderfully long time to find a suitable woman to take her place and by that time he would have returned to his regiment taking the problem away with him.

'I'm delighted to hear you say so, you need to get to know your young man better before you become his wife.'

Victoria's heart sunk to her slippers. She could hardly credit that her well ordered life had been completely turned on end in the space of one day. How could she face a man who was marrying her for her money and not because he returned her love?

* * *

The Manor was unnaturally quiet when Toby stepped inside after a leisurely ride back from Butterfield Hall. No sign of lurking servants, no children playing on the lawn with their nurse-maids, not even John or Celia evident downstairs. They must be hiding from the dowager Lady Farnham in Celia's apartment.

Knocking on the door he waited to be invited inside; as expected John was lounging in the window seat morosely reading a paper and Celia was attempting to complete an intricate needlepoint.

Toby smiled at both of them, he loved them dearly, but now he had another whose needs came first. He told them casually, from his position at the open door. 'I have something quite amazing to tell you both. In the space of a week I have fallen neck and crop for Victoria Marsh. To my astonishment she reciprocates my feelings and has accepted my offer.'

He closed the door softly behind him and left them to discuss his dramatic announcement in privacy. He gritted his teeth, if he didn't get to his own apartment soon he would need assistance to do so. As he was hobbling to his chambers he heard the strident tones of John's mother echoing along the hallway. This unpleasant old lady held the whole household in thrall. Thank the good Lord he did not have to live permanently in her vicinity. Somehow he made his way to his own chambers without mishap and was relieved when Digby appeared to assist him. He all but collapsed on to his bed and was instantly asleep.

* * *

Tonight was quite different from the last occasion she had gone out for an evening, then she had been full of anticipation, now she was downcast. Her ensemble was simpler, reflecting her mood, a modest, primrose yellow muslin with no adornment.

The thought that Sir John and Lady Farnham would be waiting to congratulate her filled her with foreboding. She must speak to the major and tell him she would not marry him, that she would face disgrace rather than settle for a loveless union.

When they reached their destination she expected to be escorted across the vast black-and-white tiled hall and announced formally. This was not to be, Sir John and Lady Farnham were waiting to meet them. Where was Major Highcliff?

In the flurry of greetings and congratulations she had no time to enquire as to his whereabouts, or to tell her happy host and hostess that she had changed her mind. She must speak to him immediately. It wasn't until they were safely seated in the drawing-room that she had a moment to ask. 'Lady Farnham, where is the major? I do hope he has not had a relapse.'

To her surprise the lady giggled. 'No, nothing like that. He has gone to try to persuade my mother-in-law to join us for dinner. They had words earlier, and she has retired in high dudgeon to her apartment and refused to leave until we have all apologised.'

Why anyone apart from Toby should be obliged to apologise was a puzzle, but Victoria thought it wasn't polite to enquire. They were all sipping sweet sherry wine when there was a flurry of activity and a small, beady-eyed old lady was bustled into the room by her beloved.

He smiled at her but she looked away, unable to meet his eyes. 'I do beg your pardon, Mrs Winterton, Miss Marsh, for keeping you waiting. Might I introduce to you Lady Farnham?'

Aunt Martha stared, round eyed. 'Good heavens! It can't be! Amelia Ponsonby, I have not seen you since we came out together.'

'Martha Finsbury, my dearest friend, what are you doing here?'

Ignoring the interested spectators the two old ladies took themselves to the far end of the drawing-room and became totally immersed in a conversation full of reminiscences and do you recalls.

'What an amazing coincidence, I had no idea that my mother knew your great aunt, Miss Marsh.'

Victoria mumbled a suitable reply but was acutely aware of the major's direct stare. She must speak to him before dinner was announced, she could not let a toast to be called to celebrate their engagement, it would be even more difficult to cry off after that was done.

She glanced up and nodded towards a small anteroom, he understood immediately and followed her there. 'What is it, sweetheart? You look so unhappy, yet when I left you, you were radiant.'

She faced him, her face stony. 'I cannot marry you, Major Highcliff. I now understand your eagerness. By marrying me you'll become a wealthy man. I have no wish to be bought. I shall never marry without love.'

She dared to look at him and her heart quailed at the fury on his face. He did not dispute her accusation, merely bowed formally. His voice chilled her to the bone.

'I accept your decision, Miss Marsh,

I shall not importune you again. Pray excuse me, I must speak to Sir John before we go into dinner.'

He walked away, his limp more noticeable, but his back ramrod straight. Why was he so angry? Was it that he had been discovered in his deceit or something else entirely?

★ ★ ★

Toby wanted to smash his fist into the wall, or go back and tell the girl he loved with all his heart how her cruel words had destroyed his happiness. How could she had thought him a fortune hunter when he was marrying her for love? He must corner John and tell him before he ordered the champagne to be uncorked. He stopped dead, sending a shockwave of pain through his damaged leg. Good grief, what a numbskull he was. Her aunt must have spoken to her before he had made his offer, small wonder she thought him a fortune hunter.

He turned awkwardly, he must explain,

put his heart at her feet and see if he could get her to change her mind. However, the anti-room was empty. He must find her and bring her back before anyone noticed her absence.

*　*　*

Victoria fled down endless passages blinded by tears. Eventually she came to the orangery, she would hide in here until she had recovered her composure. She pushed open the door and walked in. It was warm and damp, she took a deep breath and was immediately overwhelmed by the sweet scent of orange blossom and ripe pineapples. The sickly smell was too much for her, she spun and dashed for the door.

Her flight was stopped by a solid body in front of her. 'Sweetheart, I am so sorry, I should have told you that I love you, should have asked you to marry me last night. I would give my life for you, I would never do anything to upset you.'

Raising her tearstained face she stared at him scarcely able to believe what he was saying. He had no need to say anything else, his expression told her all she needed to know. She had almost ruined both their lives by her lack of trust. 'I love you so much, Toby, but I could not have married you if you did not return my feelings.'

'My darling girl, have I not been showing you, in every way I could, how much I care?'

'I know, it is all my fault. These misunderstandings are always bound to occur when we have only known each other for such a short time.'

He opened his arms and she tumbled into them. Ten glorious minutes later he pushed her gently away, brushing the last of the tears from her cheeks with his thumb.

'Darling, we must go back, dinner will be announced soon.'

She sniffed inelegantly and a large soft cotton square was pushed into her fingers. She mopped her face and blew her nose loudly. 'My love, there is one further problem we have yet to overcome — it's Aunt Martha. I cannot abandon her, I am all she has and she is old and frail.'

'Is that all? I am content to live with Mrs Winterton, don't you understand, my darling, it matters nothing to me where I live as long as we are together.'

In perfect harmony they hurried back to the drawing-room not a moment too soon. As they arrived dinner was announced and Toby led her forward. He whispered into her ear as they progressed to the dining room. 'My love, you look lovely this evening, absolutely breathtaking. I had intended to tell you, but never had the opportunity until now.' He grinned. 'Although I must admit I preferred your emerald green gown.'

★ ★ ★

The meal progressed uneventfully. There was much discussion about the capture of the gang of robbers and their forthcoming nuptials. Victoria nodded and smiled when necessary, but had little notion of what passed her lips; it could have been sawdust or the finest dishes in the land.

When the last covers were removed and Lady Farnham was about to lead the ladies to the drawing-room her mother-in-law rapped on the table. Every head turned in her direction quietly bracing themselves for whatever tirade might follow.

'I have an announcement to make. I shall be leaving here in the morning, my dearest friend, Martha, has invited me to make my home with her.'

This was greeted by exclamations of surprise and delight. The gentlemen refused to remain on their own in the dining-room and the entire party returned to the drawing-room. Immediately Toby touched her gloved hand and nodded towards the open doors at the end of the room. His demeanour did not bode well. Victoria followed him outside.

'My love, I cannot live under the same roof as that woman. Even for you I will not do it. We would be constantly at loggerheads, no one would have a moment's peace. She dislikes me as much as I do her.'

'And I cannot leave my aunt. What are we to do? I can see no answer to this dilemma.'

Behind them, the French door opened and Lady Farnham drifted out in a cloud of peach coloured chiffon. 'Ah, I've found you at last. You must come in at once, John is waiting and ready to toast your engagement. The champagne is already opened and poured and waiting your happy arrival.'

Victoria looked helplessly at Toby and he shrugged, his expression as wretched as hers. They must both make an effort to look happy, it would not do to appear miserable at such a time. He put his arm around her waist and pulled her near.

'Do you still wish to marry me if we can find a solution to this problem?'

She nodded, blinking back the tears. 'With all my heart.'

'Then we shall enjoy a long betrothal, I shall remain here and we can spend every day together. It is not a perfect answer, but at least we will know that one day we shall marry.'

'You would really wait for me? God willing, it will be many years before I am free.'

He kissed her cheek tenderly. 'As long as I know that one day we shall be man and wife, I am content to wait.'

When the glasses were raised and their health was drunk her smile was genuine; how could she ever have thought him unsympathetic? She could not imagine any other gentleman who would be prepared to wait indefinitely for his bride.

12

On the return journey her aunt was full of plans for the arrival of her long lost school friend. 'My dear, now you can leave here with a clear conscience. I shall have my bosom bow as company, but I think it would be wise not to be married until you have got to know each other better.'

'Major Highcliff is quite prepared to wait until you are properly settled.'

'Amelia is not to everybody's taste, but she and I were always good friends. She needs a settled home as much as I need a loving companion to replace you. You will not move too far away, will you, my love?'

A wild excitement was bubbling up inside, Victoria could scarcely breathe. 'I shall insist that we buy an estate within half an hour's ride. We shall begin our search tomorrow. Would you think it too soon for us to marry when we have found somewhere suitable to live?'

'No, my dear, I think that would be ideal. Good, here we are, our home at last. Thankfully, I have no wish for further sustenance, I shall away to my bed immediately. Tomorrow I must get Bennett to prepare some rooms for my new guest. Knowing Amelia she will descend on us before luncheon.'

★ ★ ★

The following morning Victoria was up at dawn. She dressed herself, not wishing to wake her abigail so early. She would walk in the garden, listen to the birds and thank God for sending Toby to her, she could not wait to tell him the good news. She had completed her promenade and was about to go inside when his horse thundered across the lawn, huge divots flying up behind him. Her beloved rolled from the saddle and tossed his reins aside.

'I could not stay away, I have decided I shall live here with you, it is madness to remain apart because of that dreadful woman. Loving you has made me whole again, I cannot live without you by my side.'

She reached out and clutched his jacket in her excitement. 'There's no need, my aunt insists that she is content for us to marry when we have found somewhere to live.'

With a roar of triumph he swept her from her feet and kissed her in full view of the gaping stable hand. He displayed such happiness on his face she could scarcely believe it.

'My love, I have decided to resign my commission, with what little I have saved and your settlement we can buy ourselves a tidy estate somewhere. We must start looking for something immediately. It won't be grand, not what you're accustomed to at all.'

She smiled at him. 'I care not, as long as we are together I shall be content.'

Her heart was almost too full for her to speak. 'I do love you and now we have the rest of our lives to get to know each other better.'

THE END